USA T
Dᴀ

Noah's NEMESIS

HEROES FOR HIRE

NOAH'S NEMESIS: HEROES FOR HIRE, BOOK 25
Dale Mayer
Valley Publishing Ltd.

Copyright © 2021

All rights reserved. Except for use in any review, the reproduction or utilization of this work in whole or in part by any electronic, mechanical or other means, now known or hereafter invented, including xerography, photocopying and recording, or in any information storage or retrieval system, is forbidden without the written permission of the publisher.

This is a work of fiction. Names, characters, places, brands, media, and incidents are either the product of the author's imagination or are used fictitiously. Any resemblance to actual events, locales, or persons, living or dead, is entirely coincidental.

ISBN-13: 978-1-773364-7-11
Print Edition

Books in This Series:

Levi's Legend: Heroes for Hire, Book 1
Stone's Surrender: Heroes for Hire, Book 2
Merk's Mistake: Heroes for Hire, Book 3
Rhodes's Reward: Heroes for Hire, Book 4
Flynn's Firecracker: Heroes for Hire, Book 5
Logan's Light: Heroes for Hire, Book 6
Harrison's Heart: Heroes for Hire, Book 7
Saul's Sweetheart: Heroes for Hire, Book 8
Dakota's Delight: Heroes for Hire, Book 9
Tyson's Treasure: Heroes for Hire, Book 10
Jace's Jewel: Heroes for Hire, Book 11
Rory's Rose: Heroes for Hire, Book 12
Brandon's Bliss: Heroes for Hire, Book 13
Liam's Lily: Heroes for Hire, Book 14
North's Nikki: Heroes for Hire, Book 15
Anders's Angel: Heroes for Hire, Book 16
Reyes's Raina: Heroes for Hire, Book 17
Dezi's Diamond: Heroes for Hire, Book 18
Vince's Vixen: Heroes for Hire, Book 19
Ice's Icing: Heroes for Hire, Book 20
Johan's Joy: Heroes for Hire, Book 21
Galen's Gemma: Heroes for Hire, Book 22
Zack's Zest: Heroes for Hire, Book 23

Bonaparte's Belle: Heroes for Hire, Book 24
Noah's Nemesis: Heroes for Hire, Book 25
Tomas's Trials: Heroes for Hire, Book 26
Heroes for Hire, Books 1–3
Heroes for Hire, Books 4–6
Heroes for Hire, Books 7–9
Heroes for Hire, Books 10–12
Heroes for Hire, Books 13–15

About This Book

Noah heard the woman's cry for help through Levi's phone, and he was already in the car and moving before anyone could stop him. He hated for any woman to be in distress, and this one sounded devastated. Having helped her once, he was determined to keep her safe, while the team tracked down her attacker.

Dianne was looking forward to her upcoming weekend seminar and even more to the few days with her friend, Ice, at the compound. Dianne wanted to talk over a business idea she was ready to put into place. Being attacked wasn't part of the plan. Neither was Noah. Still she was happy to have him as a babysitter, given the circumstances.

Only someone has a grudge against Levi and sees Dianne as a way to get back at him.

Sign up to be notified of all Dale's releases here!
https://smarturl.it/DaleNews

Prologue

NOAH WILKERSON WALKED into Levi's kitchen and sat down, hoping for a midmorning snack and more coffee.

"Hey, Noah. Even your buddy Bonaparte is hooked up now, isn't he?" Levi asked.

Just then Bonaparte walked into the kitchen. "What's this? I heard my name, didn't I?"

"Yeah, how is Angela doing?" Levi asked him.

"She's doing amazing," Bonaparte said, with a big grin.

Noah stared at him. "I haven't seen that smile on your face before."

"Hey," he said, "you haven't met Angela."

Noah laughed. "Nope, but I do hear that you were pretty resistant to the idea, before you went out there."

"I sure was, but she changed my mind pretty damn fast."

Noah looked over at Levi, just as Ice appeared. "So, you guys are running quite the matchmaking service, it seems."

"Sometimes it works out that way," Ice said, with a smile. "You interested?"

Noah thought about it, shrugged, and said, "Well, if you can find me a partner like the ones you've found for these guys, maybe," he said. "I can't say I've really been thinking about it though."

"Of course not," Ice said, her smile growing bigger.

"Nobody really thinks about it, unless they've been trying for a long time."

"Nope, not me. I broke up about a year ago from a long-term relationship and haven't really found anybody interesting since."

"What broke it up, Noah?" Bonaparte asked.

"She wanted a family, and, in the four years we were together, she couldn't conceive. So she decided she wanted to change the herd sire." They all just stared at him, and finally he shrugged, picked up his cup of coffee, and had a sip. It was the first time he'd really told the truth about it.

"Wow," Ice said. "I'm sorry. Did you ever get tested? Or did she?"

He shook his head. "I didn't. Don't know about her. Maybe she did and didn't tell me. I don't really know. But that was the reason she gave for the breakup."

Just then a phone call came in, Ice taking it.

"What's going on?" Levi asked Ice, when her expression changed.

"Remember Di?" Ice asked Levi, while listening to the caller on the other end too.

"Which one? Diamond?"

"No, Dianne from Australia."

"Oh, yeah, sure. What about her?"

"She's in Houston, and she said—Wait, Dianne. I'm putting the phone on Speaker."

"Okay," Di said, and they heard her taking several deep breaths.

"Are you okay?" Ice asked.

"I'm not sure I am," she said, with a tearful tone. "I was just attacked in my car."

"Uh-oh," Ice said. "Did you call the cops?"

"I would have," she said, "but he, the guy, had a strange message."

"What message?" Levi asked.

"Oh, good. Levi, I'm glad you're there," she said in relief.

"Dianne, are you hurt?"

"No," she said. "Well, yes, but not badly."

"Take it easy," Ice said calmly, her tone measured and comforting. "You're safe now."

"Well, I am now that he's gone," she said, with a hysterical laugh. "Unfortunately he didn't leave fast enough. He cut me."

"How bad?" Levi asked sharply.

"My arm, my shoulder, and a slice across my belly," she said. "None of them look bad. They're just stinging and painful. I'll have to get them checked."

"So tell me again. Why call us and not the police?" Levi asked curiously.

"Because the attacker, he had a message for you."

"For me?" Levi asked, standing now and walking closer to Ice. "What did he say?"

"He said, it was for—for past sins." Then she started to cry.

"Jesus," he said, staring at Ice. "Did you recognize him, Dianne?"

"Yes," she whispered. "It was Maxwell."

"Maxwell? Maxwell who?"

"Do you remember the guy who approached us on the boardwalk in Sydney a while ago? The really angry man, who lashed out verbally at the two of you? We were talking about me coming to Texas, when he ran up to us, screaming at you. Something about losing his son and it was your fault?"

"That Maxwell?" Levi asked.

"Yes."

"But that makes no sense," he said.

"No," she said. "None of it makes any sense. But it was him. He was right here, attacking me moments ago, and something about past sins was your message."

"But we didn't have anything to do with the death of his son."

"No," she said, "but remember? He wanted your help, when his son was used against him."

"And you really think that's why he's after us?"

She started to cry again.

Noah stared at the three of them in shock. "Hey, Dianne. This is Noah."

"Noah? Do I know you?"

"I work for Levi," he said. "I'm not sure if we've met before or not, but do you want me to come help you?"

There was silence as Levi looked at Noah.

Noah shrugged. "I don't want to see her alone right now."

"Where are you?" Levi asked Dianne.

"Just give me an address," Noah said to her, "and I'll head your way. What are you doing there anyway?"

"I'm here for a conference," she said, "and, when I went to the underground parking lot for my rental, wanting a break, just to grab a coffee or a quick bite, that's when he attacked me."

"Sit tight. I'm coming." Noah turned to Ice and said, "Can you get me as much information as you can, then hook me into the conversation, while I drive there?"

She nodded. "On it," she said. "Dianne, I'll call you right back. Noah is on his way."

"Okay," she said, her voice small, her tone teary. "I just don't know why Maxwell used me to get to you."

"Wrong place, wrong time," Levi said.

"I don't think so," she said, her voice getting stronger. "The way he cut me, it felt like so much more than that."

"Don't worry. We'll get to the bottom of it. Noah is headed your way."

Chapter 1

NOAH WILKERSON WAS in one of Levi's vehicles and out the front gate of the compound, racing toward Dianne's location within a few minutes. It had been instinctive to grab one of the vehicles with bulletproof glass. But, if somebody was after her, it would be hard enough to deal with all the possible issues without getting sidelined by something unexpected. Sure, it was an abundance of caution—too much, perhaps—but that wasn't a problem for him.

After spending several years working for people like Levi and Bullard all around the globe, Noah had settled back in his home country and had found that the violence was just about as bad in the USA as everywhere else he'd been. It was second nature for him to look around every corner for it. He didn't think he'd ever met Di before, but he'd heard about her from their mutual friends. Then he thought about it again, and they may have crossed paths in Australia, but he just couldn't think of the details right now.

The fear in her voice had been compelling. She was absolutely terrified. They didn't have anybody in town right now, one of the few days nobody was running errands or picking up supplies or anything. Dianne just had to hold tight, stay on the phone, and talk to Levi and Ice, while Noah drove into Houston proper. He wasn't even a few minutes out of Levi's compound when his phone rang. He quickly punched buttons and was connected into a conference call between Ice, Levi, and Dianne.

"Any news?" Noah asked.

"Nothing yet," Levi said. "She's sitting still. The car doors are locked. She's just terrified." A gentle sob came in the background and then obvious efforts on Dianne's part to regain her breathing.

"I'm ... I'm okay," she said.

"Just hold strong," Noah said. "Fifteen minutes, that's all."

Levi said on a humorous note, "Unless, at that rate, you get pulled over."

"*Naw*, not happening," Noah said. "The angels are on my side. They know I have to help someone."

"I hope they are," Di said, and then her voice gained strength. "And then I'll want to know where they were an hour ago."

Noah smiled at that, loving the grit in her voice. "Well, messages sent like Maxwell's are never very nice," he said. "And the reasoning behind all this, if we're correct in our thinking, is even harder. When a man loses somebody very close to him, somebody he obviously cares deeply for, it's understandable that he'd go off the deep end, but he can't stay there. Levi, how long ago was it that his son died?"

"It's got to be at least a year, I would think."

Ice stepped in and said, "I think it was about eleven months ago."

"So, long enough to recover from the initial wave of grief, yet not long enough to establish a new world order in your life," Noah murmured. "And just long enough for something like revenge to grow."

"Yes," Levi said heavily. "We weren't responsible for his son dying though, so I'm not sure why he's latched on to us."

"It doesn't really matter, since it appears that he has chosen us, rational or not," Noah stated. "What's interesting is that he's using transference and sees Di as a way to get at you."

"I'm thinking that must have been something off the cuff," Ice said. "Maybe he just saw Di, and it was a flashback of us together joined with Maxwell losing his son, and everything just aligned itself into this being what he had to do."

Dianne gave a choking laugh at that. "My God," she said, "that just makes me wonder how many people are out there who have a screw loose and are ready to blow."

"Well, think about it," Ice said in a calm voice. "Say he's going along in life, doing the best he can to find a new way to live, then all of a sudden he sees somebody related to the worst horror he went through, and she's sitting there in a fancy hotel's parking lot, having a happy successful life, while he's struggling, and his anger and rage just lashes out. It's a simple case of transference. He knows you're connected to Levi and me, so unfortunately you became an easy target that he could reach, instead of hitting out at the two of us."

At that, Dianne calmed a little more. "I guess," she said. "He seemed so angry."

"That's because he hasn't dealt with his issues," Ice murmured. "He's still looking to lash out."

"Survivor's guilt?" Noah asked.

"Hey, I'm sure we could get into tons of psychological stuff here. The bottom line is that Maxwell's targeting us and our friends," Levi said. "Noah, you need to keep an eye out and make sure that somebody isn't targeting you now."

"Well, this vehicle doesn't have any identifying symbols on it, and nobody knows that I've worked for you for years overseas," he said.

A thoughtful tone came into Ice's voice, as she said, "You know what? You're right. You could be the best man for this job, since you are relatively unknown here now."

"Except for a few of your guys, I've worked with," Noah said, "nobody here will have any clue."

"And the fact that Maxwell's already targeted Dianne for his anger is interesting," Ice said.

"I think either he's just warming up or it doesn't matter. As long as he can start on the fringes and hurt us, he'll be happy," Levi said.

"The question is, who might he see as his next target?" Noah asked. "Because Maxwell's obviously in town here, so who all is in danger?"

"Everyone," Ice said. "All of our team and their partners will immediately be put on lockdown."

"*Great*," Dianne said. "They'll all love me for that."

"Not if they understand what's just happened," Ice said. "It's one of the rules of being here. You'll always be on the edge of some kind of attack or another."

"You know something? I used to think the USA was safe," Noah said, with a laugh. "But it seems like, in some ways, it's just as bad or even worse than anywhere else."

"An awful lot of domestic violence is here," Ice said. "But usually that's targeted much closer to home than something like this."

"Well, I'm just hitting the city limits," Noah said, "so hold tight, Dianne."

He clicked off the phone and maneuvered through the

traffic just starting to build. He was an expert driver, and he needed to shave off as many minutes as he could getting to Dianne. He knew that she had calmed down and was doing much better than she had been, but he didn't want the attacker sitting off to the side, waiting to come back and torment her again. Because Noah had seen that happen too. Sometimes an attack happened, and the perpetrator retreated, enjoying seeing the victim deal with the aftermath and the trauma, only to go after them again. That wouldn't wash with Noah today.

Still, the traffic was just heavy enough that, for every minute he shaved off, he lost a couple more in lights and idiots. Never any way to deal with the bad drivers on the road and elsewhere, except to smile kindly and to keep going. What he wanted to do was take a battering ram and clear the freeway for his own use. It seemed like, anytime he tried to get anywhere, many more people were trying to get someplace too. And they were always in his face.

Still, by the time he drove down the designated street, looking for the hotel and the connected car park where Di was, he had made good time overall. He set up his phone again and called Ice. "I think I'm about thirty meters away."

"We just got off the phone with her," she said. "Second layer, spot D42."

"Okay, I'm going in now." He hung up, pulled into the car park, swung up to the second loop, and slowly drove ahead. When he found the spot, he stopped and frowned. He called Ice again on his phone. "Hey, what was that number again?"

"D42," she said. "She's got a dark green Honda SUV."

"Well, a dark green Honda is here, but it's empty," he said. He turned off the engine and hopped out, his phone in his hand, as he walked over to the vehicle. "No sign of her," he announced, followed by a moment of silence.

"I just got off the phone from her," Ice said. "Not a minute ago."

"And she sounded okay?" He looked around the area but saw no sign of anybody walking nearby. "The place is deserted."

"Dammit," she said.

Noah said, "Let me check inside the vehicle." He opened up the driver's side, surprised that it wasn't locked. It was empty and so was the other side, and then he heard something in the back. He flipped the front seat forward, swore, and raced around to the back, where he popped the hatch.

"I found her," he said, bending over the unconscious woman in the back. "She's been stuffed in the back of her vehicle."

"Goddammit," Ice said. "Is she okay?"

"Well, I'm checking her out." He laid down the phone, as he quickly checked her over. "It doesn't look like anything major was broken, though she has some head trauma, and the cuts she mentioned. She's moaning ever-so-slightly."

"Let's get her to the hospital."

"Yeah, it'll be easier if I take her."

"No, not easier," she said, "but faster and away from the bastard, who can't be too far away from you."

"You want to call ahead?" Noah asked, as he looked all around for anybody suspicious. "I've already got her in my arms. I'll take her in the truck."

"I don't like this at all," Ice snapped, and he heard her fretting on the other end of the phone.

"Well, we found her. She's alive, and we'll move on from here," he said. "I've got her." He struggled to open the truck door, but, when he finally did, he gently put her in the passenger seat and buckled her in tight, then shut the door, setting the car alarm. He raced back to the Honda, closed up the SUV, checked it, but he didn't see anything useful other than her purse. She'd want that. "You might want to get her vehicle combed for evidence."

"Yeah," Ice said, "we'll get it towed out of there."

"Unless the cops want it for forensics."

"I think we'll handle this one internally," Ice said.

"Well, send somebody for it then," he said. "I'm getting out of here and heading to the hospital." He raced back to his truck, turned on the engine, and quickly departed the car park. He checked on her several times, but there was no change; her pulse was slow and steady. As he flew toward the emergency entrance to the hospital, she opened her eyes, looked at him, and started shrieking.

He parked in the first available spot and said, "Calm down. Ice sent me."

She looked at him and started to shake and quiver. "My God," she whispered. "Are you Noah?"

"I'm Noah," he said. "I came to get you but found you in the back of your vehicle."

She stared at him, her eyes wide. "I just got out to stretch my legs," she said. "I was so nervous and getting worried. I knew you were coming, but, at the same time, I felt trapped inside that vehicle. It just—" And her voice fell off. "It was stupid."

"No, not necessarily," he said. "It's hard to realize that people out there are just waiting for you to make a vulnerable move like that."

"It's sick."

He saw the tears in her eyes, but she was holding them

back. "What I need to do," he said, "is get you checked over. So, let's get you inside." She stared at him and blinked owlishly. He shut off the engine, then hopped down, went around to her side, and gently helped her down.

She looked up at the hospital. "Oh, I don't need to go to a hospital," she said, her voice getting stronger.

"You need those wounds cleaned and maybe stitched, but especially someone needs to see that head wound," he said.

"No," she said. "That's not necessary. The expense and all."

"Don't you have traveling insurance?"

"Sure," she said, "but it's a pain in the ass." She shook her head, wincing. "I feel fine, really."

"That's not the point," he said firmly. "We need to make sure you're okay." She glared at him. He shrugged and said, "I'll take you in there."

"Against my will?" she challenged.

He raised both eyebrows. "If necessary, yes," he said. "You don't know what happened while you were out. You don't know how bad that head wound of yours is, and those cuts are still bleeding and should be looked at."

At his words, immediately her hands went up to her head. "Head wound?"

"Exactly," he said. "You're probably in shock and don't even know you're hurt." She frowned at him, and he said, "If you can walk in a straight line, without any hesitation, to that front door, like you've got some *oomph* and some meaning behind it," he said, "I might reconsider."

She glared at him and muttered, "Who made you the boss?" Then she strode forward to the front door. But she made it about four steps and started to pitch forward.

He caught her as she went down and said, "Case closed."

"Hate you," she muttered.

"Love you," he snickered. "Even though you're not very nice."

"I'm *very* nice," she said.

"Normally I'm sure that's true," he said. "But, when you're hurt and argumentative and cranky—which, I understand, is not quite your normal personality—I have to assume something's going on."

"Doesn't matter," she said, yawning. "I won't stay."

"You don't have to stay. We just need their equipment and their expertise to inspect your wounds."

"I'm sure Ice has the same equipment."

"Maybe, but we aren't at the compound now. This hospital was the closest," he said. He took her into the emergency entrance, and a medical team was already waiting for him. He loved that they could get such perfect service. But then Levi and Ice donated a lot of money to the place—and unfortunately donated a lot of patients too.

When the staff came forward with a gurney, Noah sat her gently there and explained what had happened. She was taken away, while he did paperwork and called in to Levi with an update. "I've got her at the hospital. They're checking her over right now. She took four steps and collapsed, so I couldn't *not* take her in, even though she really, really didn't want to go."

"No surprise there," Levi said. "She's always been like that."

"Cranky?" Noah said, with a note of humor. "I figured that was the head injury."

Levi laughed. "Well, maybe, but she tends to be a little contrary, always has been. It's part of her charm," he said.

"But we needed to get the head checked anyway, so you're right on."

"So, am I bringing her back there to the compound?"

"Yes, Ice and I have already discussed it. We need to get more details from her and figure out what's going on."

"Are you still thinking it's the same guy?"

"Well, Di remembered Maxwell and recognized him. I'm just not sure what's driving him or how far he's prepared to go."

"It seems like he's already prepared to go pretty far, especially if he's the one who came back and attacked her afterward."

"That's the curious thing about it. Why? Why not just leave her there in a panic?"

"Maybe he thought she was just way too lively," Noah muttered. "I mean, who knows what makes these guys tick? Something's broken."

"*Something's broken* is a good way to look at it," Levi said, "and, if it's broken, everybody wants to try to fix it."

"But some of these guys are beyond fixing," Noah warned.

"That's all that awesome global experience of yours speaking," Levi said in a light tone.

"Maybe. As soon as I know more," he said, "I'll call you back. Otherwise, expect us home this afternoon."

"Good enough."

"Did you pick up her vehicle?" Noah asked Levi.

"I did," he said. "That's in progress right now."

"Good." Noah hung up from the call and turned to see the doctor walking toward him.

"Light concussion and no serious side effects. She can go home with you, as long as she's not left alone."

"She's going back to the compound with Levi and Ice."

The doctor smiled. "That sounds great. Ice has a fabulous facility, with practically everything I have here, and more," he said enviously.

Noah smiled at the doc. "You know that you only have to ask for what you need."

The doc nodded. "It's just not that easy," he said. "Hiring extra personnel, training, space, and upkeep must be considered. Sometimes it's all just a big headache."

"So, no lasting injuries, nothing else except the head?"

"Yeah," he said, motioning Noah to the curtained-off rooms. "The cuts are largely superficial, except for a couple spots she needs to watch, where we put in a few stitches. If she has any further negative symptoms, don't hesitate to bring her back in again." At that, he pulled open the curtain.

Dianne was sitting up, looking a little worse for wear. She glared at him.

Noah smiled. "You ready to go home?"

At that, she looked at him. "Home?"

"To Levi and Ice at the compound."

She smiled and said, "Yes, that I would like, although I do have a hotel room. They know that, right? I don't need their largesse."

"That's got nothing to do with it, and you know it," he said in exasperation.

She shrugged. "Just so that everybody knows I'm not on the street or anything."

"You're visiting the country."

"Actually I'm not," she said. "I'm on my—I just moved back. And I'm attending this conference at that hotel, while I figure it out."

"And why move here?" he asked, as he led her back to

the truck.

"I don't know," she said. "I spent a lot of years here when I was in college. I've always felt like I needed to come back here."

"And often that's the only reason we have," he said. "Otherwise you could have stuck a pin in a map and gone anywhere."

"I could have, but I have friends here."

"Ice and Levi, you mean?"

She nodded and smiled. "And several others at the compound. I've met a lot of them over the years that I've known Ice and Levi. They've always been big on health and fitness, hence them crossing over to my area. We met when they were working in Australia on a job years ago. Ice and I just hit it off, and we've been friends ever since."

"Did you ever ask Ice for a job?"

"Wasn't sure I wanted one, honestly. I was thinking about setting up my own business, but, right now, I can't even think straight."

"And, right now, you don't even need to," he said cheerfully. He helped her into the truck and said, "Just rest, okay? We'll be about forty minutes."

"I thought you said it was a fifteen-minute drive?"

"Because I was coming to help a woman who was injured and in trauma," he said. "Now I have that same woman in the vehicle who doesn't need any extra trauma or stress from the drive," he said. "So we'll slow down and take it easy."

When he got in, she rolled her head to the side and looked at him, and said, "Since when did you become such a knight in shining armor?"

He looked at her. "I thought it was a prerequisite for

working for Levi."

―

Di burst out laughing at that. "Oh my," she said, as she grabbed her head. "That's the best line I've heard yet."

He grinned at her, an all-too-endearing grin, as he reached over, patted her gently on her knee. "Just shut your eyes and rest. Don't laugh, until your head stops hurting. And don't worry. Just rest."

"Yes, boss," she said, closing her eyes, as he pulled out of the hospital parking lot into traffic. It was nice being in a big truck like this too, high above the traffic, not feeling like she would get hit by any other vehicle. She wasn't a nervous driver, but sometimes the traffic here in Houston really got to her. And she'd driven in Ho Chi Minh City in Vietnam and some parts of Thailand that were completely uncontrolled. Yet this was very different, had an aggression to it here that she didn't like. As she settled into her seat, she wondered at the turn of events that brought her here and to this.

"Heavy thoughts?"

She rolled her head ever-so-slightly to him. "Just wondering about that strange attack."

"And yet he knew who you were?"

"Well, I presume so," she said. "After all, he had a message for Levi."

"Yes," he said, "so that makes some sense, if any of this does."

"That's the thing though. None of it does," she said.

"You know that Levi and Ice will need all kinds of information from you, when we get you there."

"I don't have anything to give them," she murmured.

"Some idiot came out of nowhere, attacked me, told me it was a warning for Levi, and took off. And, even then, I don't understand why Maxwell would attack me a second time."

"Any reason to think it wasn't the same guy?"

Her eyes widened. "Oh God," she said, "I really need it to be the same guy. To think that I was attacked by two separate people, that's too much."

"I hear you."

He kept his thoughts to himself, and she appreciated that; yet his question ate away at her. "Do you think it wasn't the same guy?"

"I don't know what to think," he said. "We just need to stay open to ideas as we get on top of this."

She sank back against the seat and wondered. The fact that she would see Ice and Levi earlier than planned was huge because they were really good friends, and she never really got a chance to visit them at the compound. It always felt like coming home whenever she saw them. It didn't matter where in the world they were; they always had the ability to make her feel like she was a part of their family. Dianne really appreciated that.

Di didn't think Ice came into that easily. Only since she became a mother was it something she became really natural at. Di had connected with Ice several years back. Maybe that had been part of the reason she had come to this part of the world. Texas hadn't been a destination that jumped out at Di as a place she really needed to go, but apparently she did. As she sat here, she wondered at the strange vagaries of fate that brought her to a place where she was immediately attacked.

"Hard to imagine," she said, "that I came this far safely, and then I'm sitting in a parking lot, and I'm attacked."

Chapter 2

DIANNE WOKE WITH a start, fear racing through her heart. She bolted upright, Noah driving still.

He grabbed her hand, saying, "It's all right. I'm Noah. You've just woken up. Take it easy."

She stared at him, as she tried to reorient herself, and then sagged back in place. "My God," she said. "I just wanted to sleep, but it seemed like that's almost worse than staying awake."

"Sometimes it can feel that way," he said, "but you're doing fine."

"Where are we?" she asked, as she sagged back.

"Almost there," he said cheerfully. "You know how to make a trip very short."

"And here I thought it was supposed to be a very short trip anyway," she teased.

He grinned at her. "And it is. We're getting there."

Di looked out her window to see that they were, indeed, at the little town just outside of Levi's compound. "I've always wondered about their location," she said.

"I think an inheritance started the whole thing here. Plus, Levi and Ice wanted a place off in the countryside anyway."

"Maybe," she murmured. "But they've sure built it into something incredible."

"That they have. Very incredible," he said. She shifted her position, reached for her coffee, and winced. "You got half of it down," he said, "but the rest went cold."

"Maybe I can get a cup when I get in."

"Are you kidding? Once Bailey and Alfred realize you're here and that you're hurt, believe me, you'll be almost sorry you brought it up." She burst out laughing. He looked at her and smiled. "You seem to be feeling better."

"I am," she said. "My head isn't killing me nearly as much." A few minutes later he pulled into the large double gates, and she looked around with interest.

"Have you ever been here?" he asked.

She shook her head. "No. I know bits and pieces from Ice."

"Interesting," he said. "I assumed you'd been here before, since you recognized the town back there."

"I recognized it from photos Ice has shared. I've also looked online and checked out the satellite feed for it. Ice always has these great stories to tell."

"They live great stories here," he said, with a smile. "It's made it a pleasure to be around."

"How long have you worked for them?"

"Years, but all around the world for the most part. This is the first time I've ever been stationed at this compound."

"It's amazing," she said, "like seriously amazing." They drove up to the front door, and he parked. She looked at him and said, "I don't think you're supposed to park here, are you? All the vehicles are over there."

"But I have an injured passenger beside me," he said, "so no way. I'm not parking over there." She looked at him and frowned. He frowned right back.

Her lips twitched. "You don't give an inch, do you?"

"Nope," he said. "Give an inch and people take a mile."

"Wow, no shortage of bitterness there."

"No bitterness at all," he said, looking at her. "Just a healthy awareness of humanity." He shut off the engine and quickly hopped out and around to her, where he opened her door.

She stared at him and said, "I could have gotten out on my own."

He shrugged. "Maybe you could have, maybe you couldn't. I didn't give you the chance." He reached up, gently grabbed her by the ribs, and lowered her to the ground, like a child.

At five-eight, she wasn't used to that, and she took a moment to gain her footing. "You're very strong."

"I am what I am."

She looked up at him and said, "That sounds like part of a song."

"Probably is," he said cheerfully. "Meanwhile, let's get you inside." She let him help her inside the front door, where they were greeted immediately by Ice coming down the long hallway. She took one look, opened her arms, and the two women hugged gently.

"Wow," Ice said, "this situation is insane."

"It is, isn't it? I had no idea that coming to this corner of the world would get me attacked."

"We feel so bad about that," Ice said fervently. "That's not what we want to happen at all."

"And not just to me, I know," she said.

"No, none of us want to see anybody attacked," Ice said. "And, in this case, we're still really unclear as to what's going on. So we do have some questions for you," she said apologetically.

"Oh, I understand the questions thing," she said, reaching up a hand to her sore head. "Any chance of a coffee while we're doing that?"

"Of course," she said, "and food. How's the stomach?"

"It's up and down," Di said. It felt so damn good to be in a place where she was safe and with friends. Ice led her into the huge kitchen that Di had heard so much about, and then Ice promptly disappeared. Dianne was immediately engulfed in gentle hugs from an older man. She accepted them gratefully.

"You must be Alfred," she said, studying the wispy hair around his face and the sheer gentleness of his countenance. She knew that he was an old military friend of Levi's, and, while she wasn't exactly sure how it all worked, it was obvious that he was happy here.

He beamed at her. "Indeed, I am," he said. He patted her back and said, "Come sit down. Sit down."

She allowed herself to be led to a large comfy chair at the table. This chair was different from the others, but it was one good to snuggle into. She sank into it gratefully and was quickly presented with a cup of coffee and a tray of goodies. She looked at the tray in astonishment.

"Where on earth did you get these from?" she murmured, as her hand hovered over the tray, while she made her selection. When she appeared to be taking too long, Alfred immediately grabbed the tongs and put three on a plate for her.

She laughed. "How did you know I was deciding between those three?"

"Because that's where your hand kept going," he said, with a bright smile. "Now you just sit and rest. You've had a terrible experience," he said. "Nobody should go through that."

"Well, it seems like that's just my day today." She looked up, and there was Noah, leaning against the doorjamb, grinning at her. She rolled her eyes. "How do you guys stay skinny here?" she whispered, as she motioned at the plate in front of her.

"We don't even try," he said, patting his stomach. "At least some of us are busy enough that it doesn't make a difference."

"At the moment," she said, "but wait until you try to stop being busy sometime."

He chuckled, sat down beside her, and said, "How are you feeling?"

"Like shit," she said cheerfully. "But this is helping an awful lot. I'm fortifying myself right now," she said, "for the questions to come." She picked up a big croissant, took a bite, and then closed her eyes with a happy sigh.

"Wow, that look on your face ..."

Her eyes flew open, finding Noah studying her. She flushed. "A little too much, huh?"

"Nope," he said, "passion is everything. Whether it's for food or other things."

She rolled her eyes at him.

"No, not like that. I just meant, like career, children, whatever it is, do it with all your heart," he said. "It's nice when I have somebody like Alfred and Bailey who can cook like they can." He added, "We all enjoy the benefits, and I do something I really enjoy outside of this."

She smiled. "And what is it that you enjoy?"

"All kinds of stuff," he said, with a cheeky grin. "But I really enjoy action and putting the bad guys in jail."

"Good," she said. "Sounds to me like there's no end of

bad guys."

"Nope, sure isn't," he murmured. He looked at the plate and then got up and walked over and picked up a couple treats of his own.

She snorted. "See? That's what I mean. How can you not eat constantly around here?"

"I wouldn't want to overeat," he said, "but this is pretty spectacular."

Bailey walked into the room, pushing a cart carrying a big water jug with lemon slices in it, alongside some scones and lemon curd. She placed the cart near the table for everyone to help themselves.

Noah looked at her and asked, "How do you guys just keep bringing out all this good stuff?"

She smiled at him. "Well, if we told you guys our secret recipes, we wouldn't have a job."

"Nope, nope, nope," Noah said. "I have no intention of that. I'm way too happy to have you around, keeping us all fed."

"You mean, fat and fed," Bailey said cheekily.

Noah looked at her in mock horror. "Surely I'm not getting fat."

"No," she said, "not yet." And, with that singsong answer, she walked back into the kitchen.

Noah looked over to find Di grinning at him. "Oh, you enjoyed that, did you?"

She nodded. "Yeah, I kind of did."

"Glad to see you stocking up yourself," he said.

"I'll need it," she moaned, as she picked up another piece.

"They won't grill you," he said softly. "They'll just ask you questions."

"Yeah, but just asking questions means reliving all that horror."

"Speaking of which," a voice said from the doorway.

Dianne looked up to see Levi. Immediately she put down the croissant in her hand, got up, walked around to him, and they shared a big, careful hug.

He held her gently, then pushed her back a bit to get a look at her. "How are you feeling?" His gaze was searching, looking for the truth that she didn't want to tell anybody.

She bolstered up a bright smile and said, "Honest, I'm doing much better."

"Well, good," he said. "And thank you for not lying and telling me that you're doing fine."

She snorted. "Since when did you ever let me get away with a lie?"

"Not lately," he said. With an arm around her shoulders, he led her back to the table. "I see Bailey and Alfred have already found you," he said, motioning at the plate of treats.

"My God," she said, "how the devil do you possibly keep them here? I'm surprised they haven't been stolen from you."

"It's all about love," he said in that same gentle tone.

She smiled and nodded. "That's what you keep telling me. I've just never experienced it to the level that you seem to have perfected here."

"Well, we're working on it," he said. Levi looked at Noah and raised his eyebrows in a comical gesture and said, "Some of our guys are still holding out."

"Hey, I'm probably one of what? Three single guys left in this place?" Noah shook his head and muttered, "Don't go looking at me."

"You're afraid of falling in love," Di teased.

"Nope, not afraid of it at all," he said. "I'm afraid of falling into what looks like love and is not."

She settled in her chair again and stared at him. "You know what? I think that's probably my problem too."

"In what way?"

"My last relationship kind of sucked," she said. "It wasn't that bad, but it just wasn't good enough to maintain. We didn't want to be alone, so we kept it going, trying to give life to something that was dead and gone."

"I've had that happen a time or two myself," he muttered. "It's not how I want to have a relationship."

"Nope," she muttered, "not at all."

Ice walked in just then, with her son, Hunter. Di looked up at the baby and held out her arms. Hunter, who had never even seen her before, immediately held out his arms.

Ice laughed. "Well, that was easy," she said. She handed off the toddler into the arms of her friend, and Hunter immediately reached out and grabbed hold of Di's hair with both fists.

Dianne let him tug and play, kissing his soft forehead. "He's beautiful," she whispered.

"Well, I'm biased," Ice said, pouring herself a coffee and sitting down at the table. "But you're right, he is." She chuckled and said, "And, while you're holding him, he'll make life a little easier for you, while you tell me what happened."

Dianne wrinkled up her nose at her friend. "Right to business, huh?"

"Yep, sure am," she said, "and the longer you evade it, the more details we'll miss out on."

Looking at Ice in surprise, Di nodded slowly. "I wasn't thinking of it from that perspective."

"Nope. Now stop stalling and start talking."

Di gave the little bit of details that she had, and, as she watched, Ice recorded it. "Why tape it?"

"So we have details to refer back to," she said. "We tend to miss out on things, or something comes up later that didn't seem relevant early on. I just do it as a matter of course now."

"Makes sense." Di turned to Noah. "Maybe he has something to add."

"Nope," he said, "I don't. When I got there, you were in the back of your vehicle."

"Any chance I crawled in there myself?" she asked.

He looked at her in surprise and then said, "I don't know."

"I—" She started to speak, then frowned and sighed. "You know? I just don't know. I don't know why I would have, except that I was terrified, and, sitting there in the front seat, I felt like I was more vulnerable and open, than if I was hidden in the back."

"And that would make perfect sense if you had," he said, "and it would alleviate the thought that somebody was hanging around, watching for you."

"But why wouldn't I have just laid down in the front seat?"

"Because you had a gearshift between the two bucket seats," he suggested.

She looked at him and frowned. "Right, I did. I usually rent vehicles without them, but this was the only one they had. I didn't even realize why because rentals don't often have standards anymore."

"Not many people know how to drive them either," he murmured.

She nodded. "But I learned to drive in the outback of

Australia, and we could drive anything there. It's a skill I've never really lost."

"That's good," Noah said. "It's not a skill that everybody has, so it's rare to find a rental with a manual transmission these days. Is there any reason to suspect that vehicle was a part of it?"

Everybody at the table shook their head.

But Ice made a note. "I'll call them and see. It will be one more thing to check off the list." She picked up the phone, while they were all sitting there and talking. By the time she got off, she shook her head and said, "It's the only one they had, and it's usually a staff vehicle. But, they had some accidents and mechanical problems and came up short on vehicles, so this one was pulled into use."

"And because I could drive a standard, I was given this one. Okay, so mark that off the list, as you said," Di murmured.

"Why were you staying at that hotel?" Noah asked her suddenly.

She shrugged and said, "The conference is being held there, so I thought it would be more convenient," she said.

"I guess," he murmured. "I just wondered if that had anything to do with it. You're attending this conference?"

"Yes." She nodded. "Hosted by the health food industry," she said, "so I was there for my work."

"Anybody else know about it?"

"Everybody back at the company I work for," she said. "Anybody who was at the conference or organizing the conference would have known about it. It was well publicized."

Noah looked at Ice and Levi. "What does this Maxwell guy do?"

"He was in construction," Levi said. "That's one of the reasons his son was taken. Somebody was trying to apply pressure to have Maxwell do a job without all the safety protocols required, and he wouldn't do it."

"So they grabbed his son?" Noah asked, incredulous.

Ice nodded. "It was a multimillion-dollar job they needed done, and everybody had refused. So they were desperate and decided to get ugly in their tactics. Unfortunately everything went wrong, and his son was killed in the process."

"Were you involved in that?" Noah asked Levi.

He shook his head. "No, I wasn't. Not at all."

"So why target you then?"

"Because he asked me for help."

There was silence at the table.

"Ouch," Noah said. "And you couldn't help, why?"

"Well, for one thing, I wasn't in Australia," he said. "Two, my teams were spread very thin. And, three, the papers said various local authorities were already on it, and Maxwell didn't give me much time, which happens with kidnappings, especially of children," he said heavily. "Ice and I discussed this at the time," he said, looking over at Ice, who nodded, "before I told Maxwell. He needed immediate help in Australia, and the local police already had a team in place." He sighed. "But then everything went wrong, and so—" He left the words hanging. "He probably blames me."

"Okay, I get that, but why attack me though?" Dianne murmured.

"Somehow he knew about the personal connection between you and me—plus, no offense here, but you would be easier to get to than one of my men—and, because of that personal link, it was just all about maximum pain."

"I've heard that phrase related to serial killers a couple times," Di said, "about them wanting to get maximum pleasure out of other people's pain."

"Yes," Levi said, "that's generally how they get their kicks. What makes their life happy and worth living is to see other people suffer. Usually these guys have messed-up histories, where they've suffered terribly, so their only way of regaining power in their life is to make others suffer, claiming joy in proving they aren't suffering anymore."

"That's kind of twisted, isn't it?"

"It's definitely twisted, but we don't have too much to go on here. I don't think Maxwell has any of that going on. I think it's all got to do with the loss of his son."

"And now he's what? Trying to make you deal with the same pain? Wouldn't that mean he would be trying to kidnap Ice or your son here?" She looked down at Hunter in her arms, his two fists in her hair, yet gently curled against her breast, snoozing.

"Precisely, which is one of the reasons we've put everybody on lockdown," he said. "That's exactly what somebody who lost a child could try to do."

She winced. "Sorry, I didn't mean to bring that up."

"Not bringing it up doesn't make it go away," Levi murmured. "We're not about hiding our heads in the sand here."

She nodded. "I'll need to go back to the hotel."

"And you want to stay there?"

"Well, I'm still part of the conference, and I'm supposed to speak tonight," she said. "I really don't want to make this trip for nothing."

"And you were supposed to stay with us this weekend anyway."

She nodded. "And I didn't have the hotel booked over the weekend either because I was coming here."

"So, you have two more days paid for at the hotel?" Noah asked.

"Three. The conference runs Monday through Thursday, but Monday is a short day, as is Thursday. Just Tuesday and Wednesday are truly full days for the conference, then Thursday morning is just a recap. So I'll check out that day."

"I don't want you to be there alone," Noah said, frowning at her.

She gave him a good frown back. "What you want isn't necessarily what'll happen," she said.

"Maybe not, but we don't want somebody grabbing you now that they know you've come here, and Ice has opened her door for you. That just adds to the theory that you're important here."

"So, if they find me again, what? They'll keep me?"

"Well, Maxwell gave you a message," Noah said, "and you passed it on, but that doesn't mean he's not waiting on you to give you another message. Especially if he knows the delivery system worked."

⁓

NOAH HADN'T MEANT to make it sound quite so harsh, but—from the pale skin, wide eyes, and shocked look on her face—he'd been a little more direct than he'd intended to be. He looked over at Ice and mouthed, *Sorry.*

Ice shrugged. "No style points perhaps, but he's telling the truth." She looked at Levi and asked, "Do you have anything for Noah in the next few days?"

He shook his head. "Now we do."

Dianne glared at them. "You'll saddle me with him?"

Noah snorted at that. "Why not?" he asked. "I've been there since the beginning."

She nodded slowly. "No, you're right there. You have been, indeed, and I shouldn't be bitchy about it," she said.

"Well, I'll put that down to still being fairly stressed."

She looked at him, smiled, and said, "Thank you for the rescue."

He nodded his head elegantly and grinned at her. "You're welcome," he said, "but I'm still coming to the conference with you."

She rolled her eyes at that. "You'll really love it."

"Can't be that bad," he said. "I mean, what was it? Natural foods? How bad could it be?"

She snorted. "Considering the time right now and the fact that I have to be back in about seven hours to give a workshop," she said, "it could be pretty bad."

He frowned. "Any security at this place?"

"Not any more than usual," she muttered. "And it's not like I can ask for more because I was attacked in the parking garage."

"I already spoke to the hotel about that," Levi said. "They don't even have cameras on that level."

"Of course not," she said. "That would make life too easy. The good thing is, I can already ID the guy, so it doesn't really matter."

"Exactly," he murmured, then turned to Noah. "You okay to go into town for a few days?"

"He doesn't have to stay there," she protested, but Noah gave her a hard look.

"Yes, I do."

She fell silent, picked up a cinnamon bun, popped a big bite in her mouth, and glared at him, as she chewed furious-ly.

He grinned and said, "That's right. Take your temper out on that cinnamon bun instead."

She groaned and said, "Now you're making me feel like an idiot."

"You've been through a shock, not to mention the bonk on the head," he said. "You're not thinking clearly."

"That's hardly the issue," she snapped. And then she immediately pulled back. "But obviously I still have a problem."

"Yeah, you think?" Noah got up. "If nobody needs me for a bit," he said, "I'll go grab my gear." He turned and walked up the hallway to his room.

So many of the staff had their own room now. Up in his, one of the rooms for short-term stays, he quickly packed up his travel bag, which pretty much held everything he had because he really didn't own much. That was good. He had several changes of clothes, and, other than that, he owned mostly fitness equipment, that he had put in the gym to use when he was here, and that wasn't a whole lot either. He walked downstairs with his bag and dropped it in the front hall.

Stone walked over, took one look, and asked, "What are you up to?"

"Hey, when did you get back from Denver?"

"A couple days ago." He nodded at the bag. "And?"

"I'll go in to Houston with Di because she insists on returning to the conference, where she's a speaker. I'm going along to keep an eye on her."

"Good luck with that," he said. "She doesn't handle a guard very well."

"Then I'll have to go as her boyfriend," he said cheerfully.

Stone started to laugh. "You know that just might work."

Di apparently heard him from the kitchen, and she hopped up and raced out. "What?"

"You either get me as your guard," he said, "or you get me as your partner." He put his hands on his hips and glared at her. "So you might as well pick right now."

"And what if I don't want to pick?" she said, putting her hands on her hips, mimicking him. By now they'd attracted a crowd, with several other people standing around.

"It doesn't matter," he said, "if you don't pick, I will."

"What will you pick?"

He gave her a flashing grin. "I'll pick partner."

She immediately shook her head. "If you want to be a partner, then I want you to be a guard."

"Too damn bad," he said. "I made the decision first." And cheerfully he picked up his bag, walked outside, and threw it into the same truck he had taken into the city earlier.

She followed him out. "You can't just make a decision like that without my okay."

"Well, I already did," he said. "I gave you a chance to pick. You didn't, so I did. Done deal. Go back inside and get another cup of coffee to-go."

"You can't tell me what to do," she said.

He looked at her with interest. "Will you ever stop arguing?" he asked.

She frowned. "I'm not arguing."

He rolled his eyes at that. "Well, maybe you should ask some other people around here if you are or are not." He watched as she turned to look at the crowd that had gathered. Flushed, she glared at him and said, "You're making me crazy."

"Hey, you were already crazy," he said, as he walked up behind her and ushered her back into the kitchen. He grinned at Levi, shook his head, and said, "You sure you don't have somebody else to go on this detail?"

"You're perfect," Ice announced from the table, where she sat, holding her son on her lap.

"I've got to wonder what you define as *perfect* in this case."

She smirked at Noah. "Ask me that question in a few days."

"Just don't try any of your matchmaking stuff," he said. He walked over, refilled his coffee cup, and sat down beside Di.

She glared at him. "You're not my partner yet. No need to be so chummy."

He snickered. "Glad you've adjusted to your new circumstances." She shifted over in her chair, giving him the cold shoulder, and he laughed out loud.

Dianne faced Ice. "Really, is he the best you could do?"

Ice nodded. "Yep. He'll look after you and keep you safe."

Dianne's shoulders slumped. "Fine," she said, "but he wouldn't be my choice."

"Too bad," Levi said, with a big grin. "He's our choice."

She sighed. "Well, can I stay here for a few hours?"

"Of course," Ice said. "If you had a swimsuit, we could go outside and enjoy the afternoon sun."

"I didn't bring my bag with me," she said. "It's still at the hotel." She frowned and looked at Noah, as if it were his fault. "I'm sure that's your fault. We should have gone to get it."

His eyebrows shot up. "When? When I was carrying you unconscious into the truck or trying to persuade you to go to the hospital or maybe when you were sound asleep while I was driving you here."

"That's no excuse," she announced, then gave him a sharp nod, turned, and looked away. When she noted Ice and Levi both grinning at her crazily, she groaned. "You know that I'll be absolutely stir-crazy by the time I'm done with this."

"You might be," Ice said. "I think he'll be stir-crazy too, so take some satisfaction in that."

At that, Dianne burst out laughing.

Chapter 3

"SO YOU SEEM well equipped here. Do you have a spare bathing suit?" Di asked her friend.

"I sure do," Ice said. "We actually have a selection. Come on. Let's get you away from going crazy with Noah and out to the pool, where you can relax, and we can have a visit."

"If I could even do some laps," she said, "it would take care of some of this stress."

"Do you want to work out instead?" she asked. "We have a big gym."

"The pool sounds nice," she said.

"What about your hair?"

"Screw the hair," she said succinctly. "If I can get a shower afterward, that'll be okay. Wash and wear, that's my style."

"What about those wounds?" Noah asked. "Is it okay to get that wet? Don't you have stitches?"

"Yes, *Mother*, but don't worry. I'm cleared to bathe, so I'm cleared to swim, not that it's any of your business."

And with that, the women left the kitchen.

Within fifteen minutes, the two women and baby Hunter were ensconced on the shaded side of the pool, while Di floated.

"Hey, this is nice," she said. "I really need to work out,

but right now I'm just exhausted. What about you?"

"No, I'm good," Ice said. "Just go ahead and do whatever you need to do to decompress."

And, with that, Dianne floated for a while, and then she swam a little. Soon she picked it up and got into her crawl rhythm and kept going. By the time she slowed, she felt the exhaustion all the way through her. She dragged her body up out of the pool and crashed on the big lounger beside Ice, who was working on a laptop while Hunter slept between her legs. "You have a beautiful place here," Dianne murmured. "I know you've sent me photos, but they don't do justice to the whole atmosphere here."

"Yeah, it's great. We've worked really hard for quite a while to get it this way."

Di sat here in comfort and felt herself getting sleepy. She murmured to Ice, "You okay if I nod off?"

"Of course," Ice said. "You're safe here."

And, on that note, Dianne drifted off.

~~~

NOAH WALKED OUT to the pool area to see the two women lying on the loungers. Ice looked up at him and smiled. "You okay to go in to town?"

"I am," he said, "and was wondering about the time. I don't know how much prep time she needs before her workshop."

Ice looked at her watch and nodded. "I was trying to give her as much time to sleep as she needed."

"As long as she's in the shade, we don't have to worry about her getting burned, but she'll need a shower, and we have to get her back in time to get her presentation materials, I'm sure."

"Well, if you've got nothing else to do," Ice teased, "I've always got paperwork you can help out with."

He shuddered and stepped back. "Oh, no thanks. Appreciate the offer, Ice, but that's the kind of training I'm not ready for," he said. "I probably should go down and get a workout in. You know? Kind of tune up in case there's trouble—if you're okay with that of course."

"Sure enough," Ice said, with a chuckle. "Come back in an hour."

He nodded and headed downstairs. In the back of his mind he was still wondering about that car park and how she ended up in the hatch of her rental. Was it Maxwell or someone else? He crossed paths with Levi, who had just finished up a workout. "I know the hotel said they didn't have any cameras in that garage level," Noah said, "but do you think anybody else may have had a camera view?"

Levi stopped and stared. "Meaning?"

"Streets outside or anybody coming or going at the same time."

"Yet we know who attacked her."

"I know," Noah said, raising both hands. "It just seems so weird, the way I found her."

"I hear you, plus she had the head injury."

Noah nodded. "And she said that could have been from the original attack, but I don't know if it was or not."

"A lot of unknowns," Levi said, "but I wouldn't let that part of it worry you."

"I just—I guess I'm concerned that there might have been more than one person."

At that, Levi slowly tilted his head. "And why would you consider that?"

"Seriously, just because of—never mind. Is anybody

close to this Maxwell guy?"

"I pulled the files, and I sent it all to your phone. And I put a paper copy on top of your bed."

"Okay, I should be looking at that now then." He hesitated and glanced at the gym.

"Go ahead and get a workout in first," Levi urged. "You know that's good for mental fitness too."

"My mind is going in a million directions right now."

"So, make it a short and intense workout and then go over the material in the briefing."

"Or I do a longer workout and you tell me." And that's what they did.

Levi filled him in on details. Maxwell's wife had died, so his son was everything. "He's in construction, has been for twenty-plus years."

"But in Australia, right?"

Levi nodded.

"So why is Maxwell here in the States?"

"I actually looked into that as well. No clue but he arrived four days ago."

"When did she arrive?"

"Two days ago."

"Do you think it was a coincidence?"

"I have a hard time with those in general," Levi said. "With the publicity for this international conference that Di is part of, I think Maxwell saw her photo, as one of the speakers, in an ad somewhere, and he traveled here specifically to target her. No proof, just my gut talking."

"Sucks," Noah murmured, "because we don't have anything definitive."

"We don't. But I expect you'll probably see him somewhere close by."

"Stalking her?"

"Just as a threat on the outside."

"Unless they followed us here."

"And that's possible too. We have a full alert on. Remember that."

"Good thing," he said. "Not too many people are set up for a deal like that."

"I suspect he won't come here in a full-on attack. It would be a lot easier for him to pick people off in town, where it'll be more one-on-one."

"That sucks too. What about the women?"

"All the partners are accounted for and are under lockdown as well. They won't leave their businesses or work without their partners or another one of us there to pick them up."

"Well, that's good to know," Noah said. He chose a machine, set the weights on, and got to work. By the time he finished his first set of reps and went through the second one, Noah was wiping down his face and shoulders.

"Other than that," Levi said, "not a whole lot there."

"I just wonder why here."

"Because Ice is here. Because I'm here," Levi said.

"Still," Noah said, with a frown, "that's a long way to come from Australia, without a plan."

"Oh, he's got a plan. Now, whether seeing Dianne changed his plan or was a part of it, we don't know," he said. "To just run into her in a secluded spot like that, I don't buy it. Even with this conference being a big international deal, maybe advertised in all countries, even then, how would Maxwell know? His forte is construction, not healthy cooking."

"I don't like the whole thing," Noah said. "I hate it

when we have no answers."

Levi laughed. "Most of the time we don't have any answers. All we ever have is more questions."

Noah nodded, and, at that point, with the briefing finished, Levi got up and left. Noah quickly finished his workout, working harder and heavier than he had before, while listening to Levi's briefing. By the time he was done, it was shower time. He headed up to his room for a quick shower, noting the file on his bed. Dressed again, he dropped off his laundry and headed back down again, this time adding the file to his travel bag.

He walked out to the pool to find Di, sitting up and scrubbing her face. "You want to shower now or back at the hotel?"

She sighed and said, "Back at the hotel would make more sense, since all my things are there." She got up, leaned over, gave Ice a big hug, and said, "Love you to bits. I'll see you this weekend." And, with that, she grabbed up the clothes she'd borrowed from Ice to replace her bloodstained ones from the attack and said, "I'll just go get changed. Thank you for the loan. I'll bring these back."

As Di left, Noah sat down beside Ice. "How's she doing mentally?" he asked.

"Honestly I think she's doing pretty well. She's aware it's still a highly dangerous situation, but she's determined to go back."

He nodded. And they sat in comfortable silence, as he stared around at the gorgeous outdoor spa area that they had built, with beautiful palm trees and plants of all kinds. "You've really got yourself an outdoor oasis here."

"We need it too," she murmured. "Just so much wrong is in the world, so we need to come home from time to time and regroup and rebuild, mending from the inside out. It takes a soul space to do that." He nodded.

Just then Di walked out, took one look at the two of them, and said, "I'm ready."

He hopped to his feet. "Let's go then." They walked back through the front hall, where he grabbed his bag and said, "Come on, out to the same truck."

She frowned. "Do you always just give orders?"

"It's easier," he said.

She rolled her eyes. "We'll get on a whole lot better if you just ask."

"Please, would you get into the truck?" he said very nicely, … too nicely.

"Okay, that's worse," she snapped. She hopped up into the truck and slammed the door hard.

He got up into the driver's side. "Maybe so, but that's what you asked for."

"Well, just go back to being an ass then."

"Perfect," he said, "that's much easier." And, with that, he started up the engine and headed back to town.

Chapter 4

DIANNE SAT QUIETLY the whole way back to town. Noah looked at her a couple times, and she noticed it, but just sank lower and lower into a fugue, as she got closer to where the attack occurred. When they came up to the parking lot, she stiffened. He reached over, linked his fingers with hers, and gave a gentle squeeze. She was surprised at his understanding and the gentleness of his touch. She sighed. "I didn't realize how much it would bother me."

"You wouldn't be human if it didn't bother you," he said. "It's all about the trauma."

"I didn't think it would bug me," she said, with a shake of her head, as she motioned at the car park. "I honestly thought I would just park in a different place, and it would all be fine."

"Maybe to a certain extent it would be," he said. "But now you're thinking about it because you're not driving, so you're not focused on everything else."

"Actually, I think, if I were the driver," she said, "it would make it even worse."

He looked at her and then said, "Maybe. Do you want me to park somewhere else?"

"No," she said, "I want to deal with this and get it over with."

Just enough firmness in her tone confirmed she was telling the truth. So often people presented this false sense of bravado, just to make sure they could get through something, but she really wanted to try getting through this, even if she failed. She wanted to find a way to get to the other side.

She watched as he pulled in and went up to the second level. As luck would have it, the very same spot she had parked in was open, and he pulled right in.

She sucked in her breath and said, "And, of course, you had to do that."

"Yep, you said you wanted to get it over with," he said, with a gentle smile.

She nodded, opened up her side, and hopped out. She looked around at all the vehicles, and many of them were likely different cars and people than when she had been here earlier today. As she had been dealing with her injuries, nobody else had even been aware. Nobody else had even been close to being aware. They had all moved on; whereas she was the one dealing with whatever garbage was still in her head. She shook her head and smiled at Noah, as he walked to the tailgate and looked at her.

"I'm fine," she said. "Just another one of those realizations, you know? That what you think is so important, so major, and so traumatic, but the rest of the world isn't even aware of—and wouldn't care about it, if they were."

"That's because they're so struck by what's important and traumatizing in their own world," he explained quietly.

"And I get that, and it's funny because I'm not even thinking about what they're going through, but I'm automatically assuming they don't care about me."

"I think we're all just human," he said. "So don't be so quick to judge yourself or others and just realize that we all do the best we can."

"Maybe," she said, "but you have to take a hard look once in a while to see the differences in the world around you."

"Agreed," he murmured. He held out a hand, and, without thinking, she linked her fingers with his and walked at his side.

"You're a nice man."

"That's funny. Just a little while ago," he said, with a sideways grin, "you were snapping at me, like a turtle."

She snorted. "Well, that turtle comment better not have anything to do with my figure," she said, "or I'll really get you for it."

"Absolutely not," he said, with a straight face. "It was entirely duty or, ah, … shall we say attitude?"

She rolled her eyes. "Something about you tends to bring out something I'm not really used to seeing in me."

"What, spice?"

"I wonder if that's what it is," she said. "I just haven't had anyone around me who changed my outlook on life, but you are managing to do that."

"Well, maybe that's a good thing."

"Maybe, but I didn't say that change was easy."

"It's not easy. It's not comfortable, and it's not terribly nice, but, on the other side of change, it always looks much better." She smiled. The two of them headed to the elevator, and, when they got inside, he punched the button for the lobby.

"I think we can go straight up to my room from here," she said.

"You don't want to check for any messages?"

"Do people still do that?" she asked in wonder.

"I don't know," he said. "You tell me."

She shrugged. "I've never done it before, and we all have cell phones now."

"Maybe so."

As they got to the lobby, he looked at her, and she shrugged and said, "Fine. Is this your instinct kicking in or something?"

"Nope, but I wouldn't mind checking out the lay of the place, so I can see just what we're up against."

Not really sure she liked his logic or his reasoning, she led the way into the lobby. "See? It's just one of those lovely big hotel lobbies. They're the same all over the world. They've got lots of little bits of seating scattered among discreet little palms or other fake trees that you sit beside and look out, as you wait for things to happen."

"I always wondered what people were waiting for."

"Usually shuttle rides," she said, "or taxis or other people to arrive. Personally I never found it a comfortable place to stay. I don't think they're really geared for that. At least not for me."

"I don't think I ever have either," he said thoughtfully, "and I've traveled a lot."

She turned around and pointed at the elevators and asked, "Can we go up to my room now?"

He nodded. "Would you mind taking the stairs?"

She shrugged and headed toward the stairs, with him in tow. When he opened the door, and they were inside the stairwell, she looked around and said, "It's a bit more isolated here, isn't it?"

"A little more but not too bad." They slowly climbed up the stairs. "What floor?"

"Five."

He nodded and kept on going.

"I clearly didn't think this through," she said, lagging a little bit. "Man, you have me so flustered."

"Ha. Hardly," he said. "It's got nothing to do with me. It's all about this scenario that you've still not quite got your head around."

"I guess," she muttered, as she kept climbing. "But a lot of stairs are here."

"We can take the elevator for the last few if you want."

"Then what will you do for exercise?"

"I'll make a trip down the stairs later."

"Oh no, you don't," she said. "I'm not a quitter." He just smiled. She groaned and said, "You did that on purpose, didn't you?"

His grin widened, and he said, "Come on. I'll race you to the top."

She looked at him in shock. "That'll never happen." But he was already running up the stairs. She followed, letting him go on ahead, but still cutting the time by half. By the time she got to the top of the stairs, she was pleasantly surprised that she was not out of breath. He looked at her approvingly.

"Now do that every day," he said, "and we'll really get you into shape."

"No thanks," she said. "There's *in shape*, like me," she said, "which is normal and average, and then there's *in shape*, like Ice, a lean, mean cutting machine."

"Very true," he said, with a nod. "And you don't need to be quite that fit."

"No, but it's not necessarily something I shouldn't be either."

"It's Ice's lifestyle, her body type, and it's how she is

happy to be physically. She likes to be at the optimum level of her own fitness."

"Athletic fitness is not something that I'm really so crazy about," she said. "Now natural foods, supplements, and all that good stuff, yes. General fitness, yes. But I don't want to go nuts with it, and I certainly don't want it to dominate my life."

"Good enough," he said. "You don't have to."

"Yet I always feel like I'm trying to justify myself," she said. "Especially in my industry because everybody's crazy about fitness."

"Well, you can be crazy but not stupid crazy about it."

She burst out laughing. "Thanks. I think you're trying to make me feel better. I'm just not sure." He opened up the door, and they walked down the hallway to her room. She fished out her card and gained access. As soon as they stepped inside, she froze. "My God," she whispered.

His arm went around her, and he pulled her back against his chest, holding her tight, while they both stood stock-still and studied her hotel room. "I never thought to check it earlier," he murmured.

"Neither did I," she said in a broken whisper.

The room had been trashed—the bed upended and cut open, all her clothing strewn around the room. Most of it looked to have been slashed as well. He pulled out his phone and quickly called management. She barely even heard the conversation. As she went to move forward, he just held her tucked up against him, so she couldn't even wander through and take a look at the damage.

Maybe that was how it was supposed to be; she didn't know. But she felt like she'd been violated all over again, her stomach clenching tight, the cinnamon bun rolling through her system. Everything was hurting; everything was on lockdown, and she felt her breathing heighten as she struggled to comprehend someone who could muster so much violence against her. And yet it apparently wasn't even directed at her; it was about Levi.

Noah put away his phone, turned her around, and pulled her tight against his chest. She burrowed in closer, trembling. "Management is coming," he said. "We won't move."

She nodded. "I can't stay here though," she cried out.

"And you won't," he said calmly. "We'll get a suite, where the two of us can be in the same place."

Relief flooded through her. "That would be so much better," she said. She dropped her forehead onto his chest. "I don't understand so much hate."

"In this case, it's probably grief and anger more than hate because, in reality, he probably has more of a hate for himself because he couldn't stop his own child from dying."

"So we're assuming it's the same person?"

"Well, I'd like to presume it's the same person," he said, "because, if it isn't, it means we have somebody else after you."

She winced at that. "No, I don't need that either."

"No, we don't," he said. "I'll phone Levi and give him an update."

"Great," she said. "Can you just call him now?"

"Yeah, I can, but I'm waiting for the manager to come." A knock came almost as soon as the words were out of his mouth. He shifted her back to the door, opened it, and stepped to the side, so the manager could come in.

He was horrified at the state of the room. He automatically turned to her.

"I don't know what happened. I haven't been here all morning, not since I was attacked in your garage," she said, with enough bitterness for the manager to look at her and then over at Noah.

"We didn't hear about that," he said.

"Yes, you did," Noah said. "Levi called."

At that name, he nodded. "Ah, that incident, yes." He shook his head. "Let's get out of here," he said. "We'll fix this."

"We'll need a room right now," he said. "Under the circumstances, I'd like to stay and keep watch, so preferably a two-bedroom suite, where she can rest and recuperate from this shock, before she has to give a presentation later today."

The manager nodded. "I can take care of that," he said and led them upstairs two floors to a large suite. Then he left, promising to come back with complimentary coffee and documentation on her new arrangements, so she could sign in here, without going to the front desk.

She looked at Noah and asked, "Did we just get bumped up so we don't create a scene?"

"Well, we'll create a scene regardless," he said calmly. "But they're hoping it won't be too big."

Slowly sagging into a large comfortable couch in the center of the suite, she said, "This room comes with furniture, huh?"

He laughed. "Yep, should be at least enough to make a difference in how comfortable you are and where you get choices to sit."

She shrugged. "I don't generally cause much fuss when I'm traveling," she said. "I just need a room. I don't need anything fancy."

"This isn't terribly fancy, even then," he said comfortably. "Besides, you couldn't stay where you were, so this makes sense."

"I guess," she muttered. "I'd still like it if it would all just go away." It wasn't long before the manager returned, pushing a trolley of coffee and desserts. She turned to Noah. "I need more substantial food than sugar."

"We'll bring in a meal," he promised her.

The paperwork, notification, and new key cards were handed off. And the manager, with profuse apologies, disappeared.

Di looked over at Noah. "I get that it's not his fault," she said, "but, at the same time, it's kind of sad."

"Sad in what way?" he asked.

"Just that it would even happen."

He looked around at the suite and said, "Pick a room and sit down and relax. I'll get some food coming." He stepped out in the hallway, leaving her to her own devices. She looked at the two bedrooms, two sections of bedrooms anyway, both kind of hooked around partial walls. She chose the one closest to her and sank down onto the bed and, with that, realized how exhausted and traumatized she was.

⁓

NOAH STOOD OUTSIDE in the hallway and called Levi about their change in location.

"How's she holding up?"

"A little more shocked, this new layer of trauma adding to the other one," he said, "which is pretty normal. I think she needs real food for one thing. The manager just brought up coffee and treats."

"Well, get something into her, maybe get her a nap."

"I may have to take her shopping," he said. "I'm not sure

if she's thought that through yet, but I don't know if any of her clothes downstairs are salvageable. I need to check."

"Do that as soon as you get her settled."

"That's what I was thinking." He hung up and walked back into the suite, finding her flat on her back in bed, staring up at the ceiling. "How are you holding up?"

"Barely," she said, rolling her head to the side. "I need to see if I have any clothing left."

"I could take a look for you." She frowned, looking just too exhausted to even move. "You don't have to come," he said, "but I figured, if I could get down there while the manager was there, I could see what we can do about your clothing. The police still need to go over the room but I might be able to grab your belongings."

She nodded and rolled her head back over and said, "I'll just stay here and relax."

"Good deal," he murmured. "I'll be back in a few minutes." And, with that, he headed out. He made his way down to her room to see the manager there, with the cleaners.

The manager looked up and frowned.

Noah shrugged and said, "We need to see if any of her clothing and work materials are salvageable," he said, pointing to the suitcases and the items strewn around.

The manager immediately nodded. "Let's hope so," he said. "I just don't have a clue what this is all about."

"No," Noah said, "you just have to wonder what the purpose of destroying things is."

"Exactly."

Noah went through her clothing. Several items were still intact. One of the suitcases was okay; another one had the corners bashed in, and several dressier evening outfits were still hanging in the closet, and her briefcase was on the floor. He looked for shoes and found a couple pairs. He packed up what was usable, then looked at the rest and asked the manager, "What will you do about this?"

"I'm not sure what I can do," he said. "Our insurance will cover it obviously, but we have to get an idea of value." He continued, "What we do is a settled amount. I can talk to the boss," he said, "but I don't know."

"Good enough," Noah said. "Let me take these back to her and see what else she'll need to round out her clothing. She's speaking tonight at the conference, which is the priority for the moment."

"Good," he said, "I wouldn't want her entire visit to be a waste."

"Me either," he said, shaking his head. "The whole thing has been very traumatizing for her."

"I'm sure." And the manager was all solicitous sympathy.

Noah quickly made his way back upstairs and carried her things over to the bed, where she lay with her eyes closed. He hesitated.

"I'm not sleeping," she said. "I was trying to find a way to get back some of my balance."

"Did it work?" he asked, in a conversational tone, as he lifted the suitcase.

She looked at the suitcase and smiled. "So not everything was broken?"

"The other suitcase is."

"Of course it is," she said. She sat up, took a look at what he had brought up, and said, "Well, I can wear one of these dresses tonight," she said, frowning at the items. "But I need to go shopping."

"Where?"

"Someplace to get underwear, for a start," she said, looking at what little was in the suitcase. "And a couple daytime outfits."

He pulled out his phone, called Ice, and said, "Where should she go shopping?" At that, he handed the phone over, and the two women chattered back and forth. Eventually the phone was returned to him.

Ice said, "Take her to Hanna Andersson."

"Good enough," he said, ending the call. He looked at Di, smiled, and said, "Now?"

"Yes, please." She hopped up, walked over toward the door, and looked at him, as if asking if he was coming.

He rolled his eyes. "Okay, *now* it is."

"Yep."

"I thought you wanted food."

"I do, but I think we'll go out and have it."

"Okay," he said. "I'm glad you're making the decisions now."

"Well, somebody has to."

A bit of her old spitfire self was a welcome sight. He grinned and walked her to the elevator, then out and into the vehicle.

As she walked out, she said to him, "I know it's not their fault, but I really don't want to stay in this hotel again."

"Let's get you through this right now," he said, "and surely we can find something better afterward."

"Well, I was supposed to go to Ice's for the weekend anyway," she said.

"Yeah, I heard you two talking about that earlier," he said. "That's good."

"Is it though? Or am I just bringing trouble to them?"

"Which is where it should be," he said calmly. "Think

about it. It's their trouble anyway, not yours."

"Well, I can't really think of it as their trouble," she said.

He sighed. "Then don't think about it at all." He looked up the Hanna's store in his GPS, confirming it was a women's clothing store. "Okay, let's go," he said. It took a little bit longer to get to the parking because he had come in off another entrance, but eventually he got parked and hopped out with her.

She looked at him hesitantly.

"Now what?" he asked.

"Well, you don't really want to come in here," she said, with a wave of her hand at the store.

"Why not?" he asked curiously.

She stared at him. "Well, it's women's clothing, for one."

Frowning, not really understanding, he asked, "Is that supposed to be something I'll avoid?"

"Well, most guys do," she said, looking up at him curiously.

"Well, I'm not most guys, and I'm looking after you, not you in the clothing," he said, "so lead on." She hesitated, then turned and walked into the store. And he wondered just what she was thinking. He picked up his phone and sent Ice a text. **So when aren't men welcome in a dress store?**

She sent back a smiling emoji. And a note. **Depends on the woman.**

Well, she doesn't get a choice.

No, in this instance, she doesn't.

With that, he walked into the store behind her.

Chapter 5

THIS PERVERSE SENSE of humor rising inside Dianne was just up to mischief, so she dragged him through the entire store. And then on to a lingerie store right next door. She did find a couple pieces, not quite enough to make her happy, but enough to get through her conference. By the time she was done, he was looking a little grim around the lips. She teased him, as she walked out of the lingerie shop. "There. That was fun, wasn't it?" He just rolled his eyes at her. She stopped, looked around at the mall, and said, "Where can we get food?"

"How about the burger joint down the corner there?" And he pointed.

She winced at that. "That will give me enough cholesterol for the whole year."

"For just one meal? I wouldn't worry about it."

She shrugged and said, "Well, maybe they have a salad." They headed toward the burger joint and sat at the far end, under an old-fashioned ceiling fan with great big leaves as blades. It was nice and cool. The waitress brought coffee, and they quickly ordered burgers, and Di had a salad on the side. She kept checking her watch, but it seemed like the time was going really slow.

"What time do you have to be there?"

"I speak at seven," she said, "and dinner is set for six."

"It starts at six?"

"Yes, it's one of those events where we go in and find our seats, the meal is served, and then, when it's time, we get up individually for our turn to speak."

"That sounds like fun." But he made a strangled sound, as if it were the last thing he'd like to do. She smiled. "I'm one of the guest speakers. So I'll give a fifteen-minute talk—ten, if I can get away with it—and then I'm giving some workshops throughout the rest of the conference."

"So, will I learn a lot?"

She looked at him, forgetting that he would attend everything. "If you'll be with me the whole time, then yes," she said. "You will."

"Good." Just then the burgers came. He looked at his plate with appreciation because the burger was big, juicy, and looked to be something he could really dig his teeth into.

She, on the other hand, felt hers was way too big for a normal bite. "What am I supposed to do with this?" she muttered.

"Bite it?" he said.

"Maybe. Only if I can squish it down though," she exclaimed. She managed to flatten it somewhat and got several bites off it to make it a little more manageable. By the time she had worked halfway through it, she couldn't finish it. She set it down and started in on her salad but only managed half of that too. By the time he was done with his burger and working through the rest of his fries, she put down her fork and said, "I'm good."

"What?" he asked, looking at her burger.

She shoved her plate toward him. "Go ahead and finish it," she said. "I have to eat in a few hours again."

"No problem," he said, as he snagged her burger. "I can

eat yours then too. I hope it's something good."

"Well, it's convention food," she said. "So it'll be okay, but it won't be top-of-the-line."

"Right," he said, "and I suppose it'll be healthy."

He said it with such a pouty tone that she had to laugh.

"I imagine it will be," she said. "That's what this whole conference is all about."

"*Great.* What would be wrong with a good steak?"

"I didn't say you wouldn't get a steak," she said. "But chances are, you'll get a load of greens to go with it."

"I like my greens," he said. "So that's not a problem."

"Good to know," she said. "Just no whining when it comes time."

"Time for what?" he said.

"Time for dessert. In case you get broccoli." He just stared at her askance. She burst out laughing. "No, I'm not necessarily kidding," she said, "but it could be the new green drinks that we're testing."

"Well, in a workshop or something that would be fine," he said. "But tonight, as a dessert? Hell no."

"Well, we'll see," she said.

He just looked at her. "Looks like you're having way too much fun."

"I need to have some fun," she announced, tossing down her napkin, "because otherwise I'd be a complete basket case."

"You're handling yourself way better than I expected you would," he said, as he popped a fry into his mouth, his gaze intense as he looked at her.

She knew that he was studying the color and the size of her eyes, her reactions, her trembling. She held out her hand in front of him. "See? I'm not shaking anymore."

He reached out, grabbed her hand with his, and lowered it gently to the table. "Good. But you can expect those symptoms to come back every once in a while, probably when you least expect it."

She winced. "You mean, when I see a trigger?"

"When something triggers it, yes," he reworded her comment.

She sighed, stared around, and said, "I guess we should go back to the hotel."

"And, of course, that's where you don't want to be, right?"

"Not really. I could go anywhere but there right about now."

"We can go to a park. We can go for a walk. We can even do more shopping." Although he seemed to choke on the word, making her grin evilly. He just rolled his eyes. "Do you have enough shoes?"

At that, she frowned and then looked worried. "You know what? I'm not sure I do. A pair of black heels were missing."

"I don't think I saw any," he said. "We can go back to your old room and check though, if you want."

"You don't think they have it all cleaned up?"

"I'm not sure," he said. "I left them at it and came and got you. Then we went out."

"Maybe we should do that then," she said. "I wouldn't mind having them back. They're nicely broken in, and they're my favorites."

"Let's go," he said. He got up and paid the bill, then escorted her to the vehicle. There, they hopped in and traveled a good fifteen minutes across town with lots of traffic, only to park in the same hotel parking spot they were in before. As she hopped out again, she said, "I don't know why you keep parking in the same spot."

"Because it's convenient, and it's empty."

Even walking through the car park gave her the shivers. Earlier, it hadn't been half as bad, but right now? It just felt wrong, as if they were being watched. He gently draped his arm along her shoulders, pulled her up close, and said quietly, "Don't look now, but we have a visitor." She stiffened immediately. He just smiled, squeezed her shoulder, and said, "It's fine."

"Says you," she whispered. "You weren't already attacked."

"Well, he's sure welcome to come attack me now," he said.

"But is it Maxwell? Is he alone?"

"This isn't Maxwell. But is he alone? That's what we're still trying to figure out," he said. "Let's go to the stairs." He walked her over there, and, as they went through the glass doors, he stopped and took a look around. She couldn't tell if anybody was still there or not. When he joined her inside the stairwell, he said, "He's gone."

"So, what then, he's hiding? You know he'll go back and trash your truck."

"Levi's truck? He might," he said, "but, if that's the avenue he wants to take, he'll bring all of Levi's crew down on him."

"Good," she said. "I can't say I'd mind it if this guy got a good thrashing himself."

"I'm sure we can oblige you with that, by the time we're done," he said.

"I don't want to be vindictive," she said, "but looking over my shoulder isn't fun and not something I'd be interested in doing the rest of my life. Even right now," she said, "just knowing somebody's out there watching me makes me feel dirty."

"Well, come on. Let's get you back up to your room." Instead of going straight to her new suite though, they went to her old room. When he got to the door, it was locked and closed. She looked at it and shrugged. "I should have kept my other key."

"They would have changed the code anyway," he said.

"Oh." She didn't think of that. She watched as he pulled out something from his pocket and, in seconds, had the door open. She stared at him. "Did you just break in?"

"Not really," he said. He led her inside to find none of the mess had been cleaned up.

"Wow," she said. "I wonder if the manager's waiting for his boss or the insurance adjustor." She quickly rummaged through the bits and pieces here and found her lipstick and her black shoes. Crowing with delight, she grabbed them and walked toward him. "Now this is perfect."

"Well, it's something anyway." Looking around, he said, "Let's get you upstairs to your room now." They walked back out and headed upstairs.

Once they were inside the suite, she said, "You know what? After that big meal, I feel like I need to crash for an hour."

"Go for it," he said. "I'll work out here in the living room."

She looked at him, smiled, and said, "Fine." Then she curled up on her bed and closed her eyes.

NOAH SAT QUIETLY in the living area, while Di napped. He

called Levi and brought him up to date, including the part about being watched in the garage. "Levi, can you check the cameras going in and out?" Noah asked.

"Yep, we'll do that right now. If we could at least figure out what he's driving, it would help. Do you think you were followed upstairs?"

"I'm counting on it," he said. "Her previous room had been trashed. We got back in there and grabbed a pair of shoes that I missed earlier, and she was happy to find a lipstick. But now we're up in the new suite."

"Do you think somebody found you there?"

"Again, I hope so, but it's hard to say," he said. "I don't feel like anybody's standing here, watching us now, but she's set to be a speaker tonight. She'll be eating dinner with the whole crowd, taking her turn at the podium, and everybody will know exactly who she is and where she is. There'll be no way to protect her."

"And she won't listen to the suggestion that she cancel, of course."

"Nope. Not for a minute," he said. "I could use a couple more men to keep an eye on the exits."

"Yeah, I've already sent two in to join you," he said. "They'll text you when they hit the garage."

"Good. I parked right where she was attacked, so they can get the lay of the land and see if anybody's hanging around."

"You expect the vehicle to be trashed?" Levi asked in a questioning tone.

"Well, if he realizes that I'm connected to you, then yes," he said, "and that would confirm exactly what we think is going on."

"It's a nice truck," Levi said in a grieved tone.

"Hey, bad guys do this all the time," he said, "and you know perfectly well that truck is as indestructible as it can get, but still it won't withstand everything."

"I know," he said. "But that one's new."

"Ha. Well, this will put it to the test then, won't it?" He ended the call. Only moments later a knock came on the door. He got up and walked to the door. He opened it quietly, expecting to see some of Levi's men there, but instead it was a stranger, a bellhop in a hotel uniform.

"This came for you at the front desk," he said, holding out the envelope in his hand.

Noah checked out his facial features and the details of his uniform carefully. Then he accepted the envelope gingerly and thanked the delivery person. He brought it back inside, set it on the table, took a photo, and sent it to Levi, who immediately called him.

"I don't like that," he said.

"It was just delivered," Noah murmured. "I haven't opened it."

"I'm not sure I want you to either," he said. "Maybe send one of the guys back with it, when they arrive."

"That's what I was wondering," he muttered. "I'll see. They're not here yet."

"I doubt fingerprints are on it."

"Not likely," he said. "It wouldn't have taken much for him to avoid leaving fingerprints behind."

"Can you see through it?"

"Looks like a sheet of paper," he said, "but again, no way to know if there's powder or anything else involved."

"Well, don't touch it," he said.

"I'm waiting on your guys," he said.

"*Our* guys," Levi muttered.

"Yeah, I hear you."

"They left long ago and will be there in a few minutes."

Noah hung up and placed the envelope off to the side. He wished he had something to put it in, but there really wasn't anything. When he heard another knock on the door, he walked over, took a look in the peephole, and saw Rory and Logan.

Noah opened the door, smiled, and said, "We got a delivery."

"I heard that," Rory said. "I'll take it and meet somebody halfway."

"It's all yours," he said. Noah walked in with the guys behind him and showed the two men the envelope. Rory picked it up with a disposable glove, took a look at it, only touched the one corner, and said, "I'll be back in about thirty minutes." Then he turned and left.

Logan smiled at Noah and asked, "Is she sleeping?"

"She was the last time I checked," he said. "She's had a rough day."

"A rough day is an understatement," she said, in a muffled voice from the door. "But I can still hear you. Who's there?"

"It's Logan," Noah said, walking around the corner.

"Oh." She looked at him nonplussed. "Why do we need reinforcements?"

"Because a lot of people will be there tonight," he said, "and I can't watch all the exits and entrances."

She shrugged and sat up, then, brushing her hair off her face, she stepped out into the main part of the suite and looked at Logan and smiled. "Hey," she said, "thanks for coming to help out."

"Not a problem," he said formally.

She smiled. "I don't think we've ever met before."

"No," he said, "we haven't."

"Levi has a ton of guys now, doesn't he?" she asked, almost enviously.

Noah looked at her, smiled, and said, "What? You think you should have a ton of guys too?"

She flushed and then laughed. "Why not?" she said. Checking her watch, she winced. "I have to leave in an hour," she said, "*Great*. You want to see if we can get some coffee?" she asked. "I need to wake up a little more."

"I can do that," Noah said. Within minutes they had coffee delivered. She looked at Logan and said, "Will you be much help?"

"Well, I hope so," he said, with a laugh.

"But you're only one man," she murmured.

"Ah," he said in understanding. "Rory is here too. He had to run an errand, but he'll be back."

"Oh, good. I know Rory," she said happily.

Noah wasn't sure if she was happy to actually have guys she knew or just to have more men around. She was oscillating back and forth between somebody who didn't care that there would be security, to somebody who was afraid there wouldn't be enough. But then it probably went along with everything else in her world right now, full of inconsistencies and oddities. But, as long as she stayed solid and could get through this, they would too.

When the coffee arrived, she sat down in the living room and slowly brushed out her hair, before plaiting it into something that he didn't quite understand, but, when locked into place at the back of her head, it looked elegant, as if a hairdresser had spent hours on it.

He shook his head as he poured her a cup of coffee from

the coffee service. "I don't know what you did with your hair, but it looks great."

She laughed. "Thanks," she said. She accepted the cup of coffee and settled back. "I really don't want to go," she muttered.

He looked over at her and asked, "Do you want to cancel now?"

She thought about it and then shook her head. "No," she said, "a lot of people are here to see me."

"Really?" he asked.

She shrugged. "It's just part of the industry."

"Well, if you feel like you need to be there and if that's a commitment you want to fulfill, then we'll do our best to keep you safe," he said.

"That's the problem, isn't it? Keeping me safe. And, after what I've already been through today," she said, "I'm really edgy."

"Nobody expects you to be anything other than that," he said, "and we'll do everything we can."

"To keep me safe," she added. "I got it." She sighed and sipped her coffee for the next few minutes, and then, when it was mostly gone, she stood and said, "I have to get dressed." She walked into the other area, where her bedroom was.

Noah looked over at Logan. "Outside of trailing her like two bodyguards, my thought is to just keep an eye on the entrances and exits."

"I do know the guy we're after," Logan said. "I think it's one of the reasons why I'm here. I was involved with another case when Maxwell asked for help."

"And you turned down the opportunity to help him, I understand."

"Well, we didn't have anybody free at the time, so it

wasn't that we turned it down as much as we just couldn't do it logistically."

"Sad that somebody would hold that against you."

"We get that more than we would like," he muttered. "People think that we're the best and that we should be there, but we don't have the manpower to drop current ops and magically appear all over the world. So, when we can't physically be there timely, we get blamed."

"Again, we're back to the reality that almost everybody is primarily concerned with themselves," he said. Logan looked at him curiously. Noah laughed. "A conversation I had with Di earlier about how we're always so wrapped up in our own lives that we think it's the only one that matters."

Logan nodded in understanding. "And I've seen it time and time again," he said. "We all have. You can't live in this world for very long without seeing that selfishness is rampant. And when there's chaos and destruction and so much of what I'll just call evil in the world, you can see why people are so focused on getting their own needs met."

"Exactly," he said. The two men talked quietly, setting up plans and communication strategies for what could possibly go wrong tonight.

When she stepped back out, she looked completely different.

Noah was momentarily stunned, as he was distracted by the professional but sophisticated outfit that showed off every curve of her body.

She smiled at him. "You can close your mouth now," she said in a teasing voice.

"You don't look anything like the woman I spent all day with," he muttered.

"Yeah, it's amazing what a little makeup can do."

He rolled his eyes at that. "If that's what makeup does," he said, "us poor guys haven't got a chance."

She burst out laughing. "I do need to go downstairs soon," she said apologetically. "I'm not trying to disturb your meeting or whatever, but I'll have to greet some of the people who are coming in."

"That's fine," Noah said, hopping to his feet. "I can come down with you now."

"And what about Logan?" she said, turning to him.

"I'm coming too," he said. "Rory just pulled into the parking lot, so I'll wait for him."

She frowned, nodded, and said, "I'm not quite ready, but I will be in a few minutes." She walked back into her little corner to the bathroom.

The two men looked at each other.

Logan grinned. "She's quite a looker."

"You're not kidding," Noah said. "I didn't see her like that all day. She was sleeping at the pool earlier but curled away from me. I—She just kind of blindsided me."

"That was obvious, and I couldn't be happier."

Noah snorted at that. "Just because a beautiful woman is our client, that doesn't mean anything," he said.

"No, but also no reason why we can't enjoy that our client is a beautiful woman."

"Sounds strange when you put it that way," he said, "but I get what you mean."

"Good," Logan said.

"Besides, you're taken. You're one of those guys happily in a long-term relationship, aren't you?"

"Yep, absolutely," he said, "and I wouldn't change it for the world."

Noah nodded and frowned. "I get that," he said. "I really

do. I'm just not sure how I feel about it though. It's like Levi and Ice are running a matchmaking service."

"Depends on whether you're part of the matchmaking world or not."

"Did they matchmake for you?"

"Nope, but I was one of the first who settled into a more traditional domestic life," he said. "At least by our standards anyway. I came to join them on a job," he said, "and that's where I found her, but, hey, I don't care how it came about. It's a good deal for me."

"Ah, but is it a good deal for her?" Di asked, as she came around the corner. This time she was ready. She had a small purse with her and her heels on. She looked at the two men. "It's time for me to go."

Just then Logan's phone went off. He checked it and smiled. "That's Rory. He's down in the lobby."

The three of them headed for the door, and, as the men walked to the stairs, she shook her head and said, "Oh, hell no, I'm not doing all those stairs in these heels."

Noah looked at her shoes, and he nodded. "Fine, I'll go down in the elevator with you." Logan stepped in with them.

She looked at the two of them. "You can go anywhere you want, you know?"

"We're here to keep an eye on you," Noah said. "So just deal with it and don't be difficult."

She groaned. "There you go again."

"I'm not doing anything," he said.

"Neither am I," she shot back in exasperation. "I was just trying to let you off the hook."

"Well, you can't let us off the hook," he said. "We're on the hook until we transfer you back to Levi and Ice's place."

"Right," she said, stiffening her spine and glaring at him.

"Fine, if you want to be that way." In the background, Noah heard Logan snickering. She turned, looked at him, and asked, "What's so funny?"

"You two," he said.

"That's not fair," she said.

"Why not?" he said. She glared at him too.

Noah said, "See? There's no winning with her."

"Don't be difficult," she admonished.

He just looked at her, shook his head, and said, "You're the one who's being difficult." Her eyes welled up with tears, and he immediately groaned. "Sorry."

"You should be," she said, sniffling back her tears. But her back was ramrod stiff as they got off the elevator, and she headed for the conference rooms.

He hadn't even looked to see where they were. As he followed her, he wasn't happy with the location. "I knew this place had a conference setting, but I didn't realize that you wouldn't be in the main conference hall."

"Tonight, it's supposed to be in a smaller, more intimate setting," she said. "At least at first. It opens to other attendees later."

He nodded. "Okay, I didn't know we had a change of venue either."

"It's always like this," she said, with a wave of her hand. "Nothing's changed."

"Maybe, but it wasn't clearly laid out that this is where you would be."

She glared at him. "You'll just have to deal with it."

He laughed. "I will," he said, loving that she could throw his own words back at him. He looked over to see Logan and Rory following a little bit behind. As they went into the smaller room that she talked about, he noted it would still hold a good eighty-plus people. "Well, it's hardly small," he muttered.

"Definitely smaller than where we'll be tomorrow," she said. As she walked in, she was greeted by several other people, who obviously knew her well. She was immediately engulfed in hugs. He was half engulfed himself, as everybody assumed that the two of them were together. He didn't dissuade anybody of the idea and just kept her close.

Finally she separated from him a little and said, "I need to go up there now." He nodded, leaned over, and kissed her gently on the cheek.

She looked at him. "What's that for?"

"Since everybody seems to assume that we're together," he said, "it seemed like the thing to do."

She flushed and walked away. But he was happy because it had brought a bright sparkle to her cheeks. She wasn't quite aware of her surroundings, and he wanted to bring her back to a sense of where she was. He watched the room, even getting up to stand at the back to keep an eye on everybody and their reactions. He didn't see anything that looked untoward. Nobody looked at Di like they were furious or panicking or even studying her too intently.

They all appeared to be old friends. And that was even more disruptive because he couldn't tell who was a problem and who was not. He knew he probably wouldn't find any of the suspected guys in here, even the stalker from the parking garage, and that was fine and dandy, but that didn't account for the possibility that Maxwell could be utilizing somebody else to cause Di harm. Or had hired somebody else to kidnap her for him.

If it got too hot for Maxwell to be around personally, it only made sense that he might bring somebody else in on this. But then Noah was thinking like the same predators that he often hunted. And they weren't always that complicated. Lots of times they were very simple. They wanted what they wanted and wouldn't take no for an answer.

From there, it just got ugly, but it wasn't that hard to figure out.

Chapter 6

IT WAS NICE to be back in her world and feeling like she was in control again. Dianne couldn't explain how unsettled the day had been so far and how it felt to have her world tossed up in the air and dropped and how wrong it all seemed to be. She came to the States every year for this conference. She had one more ulterior motive this year because she was moving back, spending at least a year or two in the US as she planned to set up her new business, wondering about getting closer to Levi and Ice, especially since she had made no close friends in Australia.

And now that the attack had happened in the very place where she was relocating, it gave her a very unsettled feeling. But here among her work friends and everybody in the industry that she knew so well from all over the world, it was just a lot of fun. Also she was back in control and where she belonged.

By the time the evening wound down, and they stood around, having drinks, and plates of hors d'oeuvres were handed out, she was accustomed to having Noah settled in beside her. If his hand wasn't on her shoulder or her arm hooked into his, it was an odd moment. And it felt natural, like they were meant to be that way.

Several people had expressed surprise at her partnership, but she had just introduced Noah naturally, with a smile.

There had been no condemnation, but he was a hell of a specimen and in way better shape than she was, and yet she was in damn fine shape. Maybe not in the fighting kind of shape that he was in, but it would be hard to find anyone who would have argued with her physical condition.

Although today's traumas had really set her back. She didn't want to let it, but it was hard. Still, by the time the evening wore down, she felt much more relaxed.

He smiled at her and said, "You're doing great."

She beamed and then confessed, "The wine is really helping too."

He chuckled at that. "We can have a bottle up in our room later, if you want."

"That's tempting," she said, "very tempting."

"We can do more than be tempted," he said. "Anything that makes it work for you."

"That's good to hear." She smiled.

Finally she said her goodbyes, and they walked out of the main room. "I didn't see Rory or Logan anywhere," she said.

"They were there," Noah said, "checking out the whole place, not just the room we were in."

"And you were in there, so they weren't needed." He just smiled at her and didn't say anything. She shrugged. "I gather you all know what you're doing, so it doesn't matter."

"Exactly," he said.

"And are they still out there watching?"

"They will be, until I let them off the hook, when we're back in our room."

"And then what? We're not expecting another attack on the room, right?"

"No, I really don't think so," he said. "It would be too obvious and a little hard for him. By now he also knows I'm here full-time, so it's not just a simple case of attacking a lone woman."

"No, but, if he comes with a weapon," she said, "you can take a bullet just as easy as the next guy."

"Maybe," he said, "but I hope not. I hope I'm not even close to being just as easy as the next guy."

"Ha, you know what I mean."

"I do, and I appreciate the concern, but it's okay."

She frowned at him. "I'm not so sure that it's okay, but I'm in a nice mellow haze from the wine, so I want to go to sleep and have a good night and forget about it."

"It's a long day tomorrow, isn't it?"

"Yeah, the first workshop starts at eight," she said, "and we go until at least four tomorrow night." He winced at that. "And, yes, you'll be with me the whole time," she said mockingly.

"I was thinking about you actually," he said. "That's a long day."

"I'm used to it," she murmured, "and it is what it is."

"Maybe, but that doesn't make it any easier," he said.

She frowned, thinking about it, and nodded. "No, you're right. It doesn't, but it's all good."

At their suite, he unlocked it, did a quick sweep, and then let her inside. He locked the door behind her and said, "Now get yourself to bed."

"And here I thought a bottle of wine was in it for me."

He laughed. "I did promise you wine, didn't I?"

"Yes, but maybe I've had enough," she said.

"You decide," he said. "If you want a couple more glasses, we can have a carafe sent up. Or even a bottle."

"No." She yawned and said, "I think I'll probably sleep just fine now."

"Final answer?"

"Sleep," she said, heading toward the bathroom. When she came out, she looked even more tired. "Definitely sleep," she said, yawning again. She walked to her bedroom, called out, *Good night*, then headed to her bed and crashed.

❦

NOAH WOKE UP the next morning early, before 5:00 a.m. Something had woken him up, but he wasn't exactly sure what, and then he heard somebody down the hallway. It's weird how you heard just footsteps because it was right outside his bedroom. He hopped to his feet and, still wearing just his boxers, silently raced to the front door. The footsteps were stealthy as they approached the door. Even as he watched, the handle wiggled. He immediately jumped on the handle, popped it open, and found a teenager—or a young adult maybe—outside. Noah grabbed him by the throat and slammed him up against the wall.

"What the hell are you doing coming into this room?" The kid choked and gasped and swung wildly at him. Noah let him down, so his feet touched the floor, long enough to catch his breath. "Now talk to me," he said, "before I knock your lights out and be done with it."

The kid took several long slow deep breaths, but his eyes flickered wildly in fear.

"I don't give a shit either way," Noah said. "Tell me, right now, and it better be the truth."

"I was paid," he said, "to slip this under your door."

"But you weren't going under the door," he said. "You were trying the doorknob."

At that, the kid panicked, barely spluttering out, "He said, if I couldn't get it under the door, to just open it."

"Hotel doors lock automatically, dumbass." The kid likely didn't know anything important and was just trying to make a break for it. "Who hired you?"

"Just a guy from outside," he said.

"Meaning?"

"Just a guy," he said, stuttering, looking longingly at the hallway and his closest exit. "He gave me a hundred bucks. I need the money, man."

"I want a description." Noah stared at the kid, as his mind seemingly went blank because he just looked at Noah with that oddly vacant look on his face.

"I don't know. He was just a guy."

"As tall as you?"

"Taller."

"Dark hair, no hair?"

"Dark, but not much of it. He was skinny. And he talked kind of weird."

"Like what? Weird how?"

He shrugged. "Like he had marbles in his mouth."

"That is weird."

"Right? That's what I thought."

"You still haven't explained why you tried the door."

"He told me to try it, if I couldn't get the thing under the door."

"You know it'll be locked, so it doesn't make any sense to try it."

"Maybe he was just checking or testing me. I don't know," he said. "I need to go now. I've got my hundred bucks, so I need to go."

"Not until I get a picture of who you are. And I want to confirm your ID."

"That's not fair," he said, "I didn't do anything."

"Like hell you didn't. You just tried to break in to a hotel room."

"No, no, I didn't," he said. "I wasn't trying to break in at all. I just wanted to give you this." He held out the envelope.

"BS," Noah said, grabbing the envelope. But then he quickly snagged the kid's wallet—knowing he wouldn't run without it—snapped a photo of his ID, along with one of the kid's face, then Noah said, "Get lost. Next time don't take any money from strangers for shit like that. It'll only cause you trouble."

"I won't. I won't." And the kid literally ran down the hallway.

Noah stepped back into the hotel room and closed the door.

"What was that all about?" Dianne asked, as she stepped out of her room.

He turned. She wore a tiny nightie that stopped just at her hips, leaving long smooth legs exposed—gorgeous legs to go with a gorgeous body. He swallowed hard and said, "Do you want to put on some clothes?"

"Don't you?" she said, with a nod toward him in his boxers. "I'm totally fine." She gave him a wicked grin. "I'm comfortable," she said in a smooth tone, as she walked over to the couch and flung herself down into the corner. "Now what the hell was going on out there?"

"We had a visitor. Somebody tried the doorknob and supposedly was paid one hundred bucks to put this under the edge of the door."

"If he was supposed to put it under the door, why turn the handle?" she reasoned.

"Exactly what I asked him," he said, "and got the answer

that he was supposed to try it."

She stared at him. "To make it look like you were getting a break-in?"

He shrugged. "Just messing with us maybe," he said.

"Still sucks," she murmured. She rubbed the sleep out of her eyes. "What time is it?" she asked, stifling a yawn.

"Not yet five."

She winced. "*Ugh*. A little too early to stay up and a little too late to crawl back into bed."

"You can go grab another hour, if you want."

"No," she said, "I'm better off to just wake up and be awake for the rest of the day."

"The same for me," he said. "Are you ready for coffee? I can order some up."

"Absolutely," she said. "I'll go get a quick shower."

He watched as she left and quickly phoned Levi, his sleepy voice on the other end confirming Noah had woken him too. He said, "We just had a visitor."

Levi came wide awake. "What kind of reception did he get?"

"Pretty poor," he said cheerfully. "He said he was supposed to put an envelope under the door."

"Well, that first envelope just had a message," he said, "about watching our back. So no poison involved."

"Well, maybe this is something similar," he said. "I just didn't want to take a chance with it."

"No, we can't take any chances. I'll send somebody to collect it."

"Good enough," he said. "We'll stay up, now that we are. Talk to you later."

He hung up from Levi, phoned for coffee, and then sent Logan and Rory texts about their early guest. Then he pulled up his laptop and started searching the delivery guy. He found out that he was literally just a kid. He'd graduated high school a year ago and had been working at odd jobs ever since. One hundred bucks to him probably seemed like gold.

Noah stared out the window, pissed that so many messengers were out there that you never knew which message would be the one that blew up in your face and which messenger was the one who wouldn't end up being quite so innocent after all.

Chapter 7

DIANNE STEPPED OUT of the shower, feeling a whole lot better and a lot less groggy. It wasn't exactly the way she wanted to wake up, hearing Noah slamming somebody against the wall, knowing immediately it was an attack on their hotel room. She didn't even know how to begin to thank him for being here with her, and, even though she was getting cheeky and giving him a bit of guff, it was more of a defense mechanism than anything. She didn't want to be alone right now and couldn't wait until this conference was over, and she could go to Ice's for the weekend.

After that, she didn't know what to do with her life, and it was partly what she wanted to discuss with Ice. They had both been talking about it over the last few years, and this was the first time Dianne had ever planned to stay for a visit here, being the first time she'd seen the compound in person. She and Ice and Levi met up all over the world when their paths crossed. But now, she was thinking about making a change and not heading back to Australia.

She'd also been offered a franchise opportunity and wanted to discuss that with her friend as well. Ice was hell on wheels when it came to business. Dianne didn't really have anybody back home to talk to about it. This conference was one way of seeing if she could utilize any connections here. She wrapped her hair up in a towel and quickly dressed for the day in the clothes that she would wear to the conference. She just held off on the makeup and her blazer. As she stepped out into the other room, she was still toweling the water off her hair. "Did the coffee come yet?"

Too bad, Noah had gotten dressed himself. She was used to fit gorgeous males, but Noah had something special that set him above the rest. It was hard to define, but he had this smooth self-confidence, not arrogance, but an internal power of someone who's seen a lot and who knew his capabilities and was comfortable with them in this world.

"It's on its way," he said, without lifting his head from the laptop.

"What are you doing? Tracking the poor kid paid to deliver that message?"

He looked up, smiled, and said, "We have to check out every lead."

"It's still all about the one guy," she said. "It's all about Maxwell."

"Well, it's all about you, but, therefore, it's all about him too."

"Now that Rory and Logan are here," she said, "won't all the attention transfer to them?"

"I hope so," he said. "I really do."

She looked at him. "I thought they were your friends."

He burst out laughing. "They are, but they also know how to take care of themselves," he said. "So, if they become the target, I have much less to worry about. Because then Maxwell won't be coming after you."

"Unless he gets through them," she said quietly. "I know you guys all think you're invincible, but you're not."

He gently smiled at her. "No, we're not, and we don't take it for granted. But what we are is very good at defending ourselves."

"Yes, but remember. Bullets don't care," she said. Just then came a knock on the door.

She made a strangled exclamation and immediately stepped back.

He looked at her and said, "It's probably the coffee. Remember?"

She nodded. "Yeah, I do," she said, "and that just proves I'm a mess."

"That's all right," he said. "You have every right to be a mess. Just relax. This was a rough start to the day, but it'll get better from here on out."

When he said it was a rough start, he was right. A shower, several cups of coffee, and pulling together everything for the first workshop of the morning should have put her back on track, but instead it felt like it would be another ugly day. She had to shake herself out of this mood. She knew that, as soon as she got busy and hooked up with all the people downstairs, she would shake off this fugue. Soon she was ready to go.

As she opened up the door to the hallway, Noah was right behind her. They walked down to the elevator, and she stood there, undecided. Since she was dressed more casually right now, he immediately nudged her gently toward the stairs. She looked at the stairs, back at him, and said, "I know it's good for us."

"It will also make you feel better," he said.

She shook her head. "How does doing something that you don't like doing make you feel better?"

"Well, you'll feel better because it will get your blood pumping and releasing endorphins," he said. "Besides, you don't really hate doing stairs. I don't buy it at all. That's not you."

"No, that's true," she admitted. "I'm just tired."

"And with good reason," he said. "When this is over, just remember. We get some downtime at Levi and Ice's."

"Trust me. That's what's keeping me going."

"You'll feel better as the day gets going."

She yawned and nodded. And, sure enough, by the time they hit the bottom of the stairs, she had a smile on her face.

He grinned at her. "See?"

She rolled her eyes. "I knew I'd feel better," she said, "but part of me begrudges having to."

He chuckled. "It's all good."

She looked around and said, "What about the other two?"

"They're here," he said in that mysterious tone. "I already handed off our second delivered message to them. One of them is handing it off for Levi to inspect."

She shook her head. "But do I greet them? Do I say anything?"

"You can. Why not? You'll know a few hundred people here, won't you?"

"Yes," she said, admitting that with an odd look. "Because you don't even think about how many people you actually know until you come to a conference like this."

He looked at his watch and said, "You've got about ten minutes."

She winced. "In that case, I need to move it." With that, she swept ahead of him down the hallway, avoiding the crowds already pooling out in the lobby, then snuck into one of the side rooms. He kept up with her, as she was at the front, organizing the presentation and the papers she had set up for this morning. As the gong in the lobby rang for 8:00

a.m., signaling the start of the seminar, she turned and watched, as the crowd moved in, and the room filled up.

Pretty soon the seats were nearly full. She scanned the crowd, a smile on her face, as she waited for the last of the attendees to come in. She hated being interrupted, but it was a fact of life in these places and with this type of event. As soon as it calmed down, her gaze roamed around the room, searching for Noah but couldn't find him. She felt her heart race, as she kept looking and looking, even as the crowd waited expectantly. Finally she caught sight of him in the very back. She took a long slow breath and flashed him a bright smile.

"Good morning, everyone." And that's how she started the session. It went on for hours, and, by the time they had a coffee break, the energy in the room was high. The audience had a ton of questions, but she finally managed to break it down and say, "Next, we'll have a twenty-minute break, and refreshments are available out in the lobby. This is your chance to get up, to stretch your legs, to dance on the spot, or to do whatever," she said. "We'll reconvene here in twenty."

And, with that, she stepped away. The room immediately erupted, as people got up and headed for the exits and the bathrooms and the coffee, and she understood the sentiment. But, for her, there would always be that rush of people who came forward, instead of leaving. And, sure enough, she was very quickly surrounded by a dozen people; some she knew, and some she didn't. She quickly greeted those she did with hugs and greetings, smiled at the others, and answered as many questions as she could, only to find Noah standing at her side. She looked up at him.

"Come on," he said. "You need a break too." She made

her excuses, and he led her out to a smaller hallway. "What's down here?" she asked curiously.

"Well, a bathroom, for one."

"I could definitely use that," she admitted. She quickly dashed into the restroom, while he waited outside. By the time she was done and had splashed some water on her face, fixed her hair, and stepped out, she felt a bit brighter.

"You're holding up pretty well," he said.

"At events like this," she said, "you feed on the energy of the group. And, so far, everything's good."

"That's good to know," he said. "Do you want me to grab you a coffee?"

"I'm not so sure," she said, checking her watch. "We've already used up a lot of time."

"We have time," he said. He took her back around that small hallway, then through another door, which took her to the side of the lobby. And right there was a coffee service.

She crowed in delight. "Man, I should have you with me all the time. I don't know how you found this out. I've been to this hotel a couple times, and I didn't know about that entrance and exit."

"There are always extra hallways for the staff to move through to the main hallways," he said.

She poured herself a coffee and looked up at him. He nodded, and she poured him one too. As she turned to hand it to him, she found him over at a plate of offerings, quickly selecting something for each of them.

"I don't have much time," she warned, but she stared at the cheese and berries with longing and then quickly scarfed down a few of each.

He laughed. "How about a croissant to hold all that down?"

She took half of it and moaned in delight. "Oh, my gosh."

They walked back into the seminar room to see most of the people had reconvened, but still plenty of seats were empty, people still milling around. She walked up to the front podium, where she finished her snack. Noah grabbed the empty plate and headed for his spot at the back of the room. She called out her thanks, as he walked away. He lifted a hand in acknowledgment and kept on going. She knew that some people, particularly those who she knew so well, were watching them, probably curious and wondering what each of them were up to.

She had never shown up with a partner before, so this was a first for her too. The rest of the day continued pretty much on the same note. Every time there was a break, Noah was at her side. She sat with him at lunch, even though she hadn't made any arrangements for him to attend, so that was a concern. But the staff never said a word, as he sat calmly beside her, during the whole thing.

"Are you even allowed to be here?" she leaned over and asked.

He whispered back, "Yes."

She smiled and settled in to enjoy her lunch and the conversation at the table around her. They usually did the seating on a casual basis, but often, in conferences like this, they gave you a seat assignment, so that everybody was mixed up, and so that you didn't just sit there with the same group of friends all the time.

She had a short stint in the afternoon; then she had a couple hours off. After lunch, she had a break. She stepped out into the lobby and took a long slow deep breath.

"Now," he said, "do you want to go outside for a bit, or

would you rather go up to your room?"

"I'd really like to go up to my room," she murmured.

"Just for a few minutes to relax, away from all these people."

"Let's go." Quickly they made their way back up to the room.

When the door shut, she felt all the stress dropping from her shoulders. She turned and looked at him. "I didn't realize how much stress I was under, until we got back here."

He nodded. "There's just that feeling that something is likely to go wrong," he said, "so you're constantly worried, even though you do your best not to show it."

"Am I showing it?"

"No, you're not showing it at all," he said. "You're doing fine."

"I'm glad to hear that," she said, "but I don't feel that way on the inside."

The afternoon progressed fairly calmly. At five o'clock, after her last session of the day, she felt the fatigue of always looking out and around hitting her. She was supposed to have been done earlier but someone else hadn't shown up for a session, so she had covered it. Now she felt the pressure and was rather desperate to go to her room and chill. She headed to the elevators, only to find Noah at her side. "I almost forgot about you," she admitted.

He laughed. "Well, I won't take that as an insult," he said. "At least this time."

"It wasn't meant as one. I was just feeling the pressure to get out of there, after taking on the extra seminar and all," she said, the fatigue, in spite of all her efforts, easily showing.

"Time for you to have a break."

"Well, that's the plan," she said, and she yawned.

"It might be a good chance to get yourself a nap."

"Sounds good to me. Did you guys find anything?"

"Nope, nothing yet. Levi checked the second message. Not laced with drugs and basically the same message."

"But the kid delivered it. Maxwell could already be long gone," she said.

"Hope so."

But something odd was in his voice. She looked at him. "You don't believe that though, do you?"

"No, I sure don't," he said.

Her shoulders sagged. "You could have let me at least hope for a little while."

"No point in doing that," he said gently.

"I guess," she said. "But I would really like to have all this over with."

"I know you would, but we're not to that point yet."

"No," she whispered. As they walked into her suite, she collapsed on her bed and said, "I am so done."

"Lay back," he said, "kick off your shoes, and curl up for a while. I'll stay here for a bit until you're out."

"I'm not going to argue with you. At least I should nap that way." She followed his instructions and was asleep within minutes.

˜

NOAH ALWAYS WONDERED how somebody could sleep like that. Dianne had crashed like a baby. He did it when he needed to for power naps, for work, when they were out on missions and had but a few hours and nothing else, but he had never really seen it in other people. She did it with such trust and innocence that it amazed him even more. He was happy because it meant that she trusted him; otherwise she couldn't sleep like that, but, at the same time, it was interesting to see somebody else conserve her energy and make good use of downtime, like she was.

His phone rang at that point. It was barely loud enough for him to hear it, but he looked to see it was Levi. "Hey."

"How is she?"

"She's just now crashed back in her room. She's done with the first full day of the seminar, but these things have a nighttime schedule too."

"How did it go?"

"Fine," he said. "There's been absolutely no sign of anyone or anything the least bit off."

"Odd," he said. "Those cases are the worst, aren't they?"

"They sure are," Noah said cheerfully, "because you keep looking, you know somebody's out there, but they're just playing the waiting game, leaving you with nothing to do but play along. You get stressed and frustrated because you're forever looking over your shoulder, and, just when you get calm and think it's all safe, well, that's when they jump."

"And that's the plan with her, I'm sure," Levi said.

"So far," Noah went on, "there doesn't appear to be any disruption in the seminar itself. We've split up the guest list, all the attendees and all the speakers, and we haven't found anything that might be connected. Rory and Logan are currently going over the actual attendant and staff list, looking to see if we can come up with any cross-referencing there."

"They did send some names back here for further checks," Levi said. "So far, we haven't come up with anything either."

"No, it appears to all be related back to this one Maxwell guy."

"That's fine," he said. "Way better that it's a single attacker than a whole team."

"I get that," he said, "but Maxwell hired that kid, could be doing that now. Makes it much harder to determine if anybody else is here, standing in for Maxwell."

"No sign of the kid?"

"Nope."

"No sign at all?"

"No," he murmured. "I have been keeping an eye out for him."

"We've tracked him down. He's normally a pizza delivery guy, was in college—until he couldn't make the next term's payments—and he's been doing odd jobs since."

"Right. So just a kid trying to get back into school."

"As far as we can tell, yes," he said.

"Well, at least his story checks out."

"But that doesn't mean the next guy's will."

"I guess the question is, how many times will Maxwell use other people, and what is the motive behind it?"

"Well, he keeps his distance, doesn't he?"

"Except for when it came to attacking her, with a knife of all things."

"Yet he didn't seriously hurt her, which is another valid point. Because he isn't trying to fatally hurt her, so it really was as much a warning as anything else."

"But it scared the crap out of her," he said, his voice turning hard. "So hardly an acceptable tactic."

"No, but something to keep in mind. He didn't shoot her." And, with that, Levi rang off.

Noah stared across the room, where she still slept soundly. It was a good point on Levi's part, but often, when warning attacks happened, they were followed up with something more violent and more vicious. It's like the attackers were testing the waters, then got angry because the object they were after wasn't paying attention. So the next attack would come on harder and stronger. Noah needed to make sure that didn't happen this time.

As he sat here, going through the notes that Levi had sent him on the kid, he thought how Dianne would probably want some coffee when she woke up, so he quickly ordered up room service. When it was delivered, it was brought in by Rory.

"How is she doing?"

"She's napping right now, since she's off until dinner tonight, having agreed to an unexpected session as one presenter isn't feeling good."

"Good," he said. "We've done a full check and run all the license plates," he said. "Absolutely no sign of anybody suspicious at the moment."

"I know, and that's more worrisome than ever."

"No sign of Maxwell, no facial recognition popping up anywhere. He is in the city, as far as we know, but he's hiding out."

"Well, he also doesn't know if the cops are after him."

"I don't think she contacted them, did she?"

"No, she contacted Levi instead."

"Which is a good call on her part, yet the cops probably do need to be aware."

"You could check in with Levi and see if they brought them in on it."

Rory nodded. "I'll do that." Looking around, he said, "I guess we'll leave you here then, keeping an eye on things for the rest of the evening."

Noah nodded. "There's a dinner and then another speaker address tonight."

"So," Rory said, "she should be done at maybe what? Nine o'clock or so?"

"Yes," Noah stated.

"Then," Rory added, "we will hand her off to you in this room as long as you stay here."

"That's the plan," Noah said, "at least I can protect her here."

With that, Rory nodded and left. As soon as the door closed, Di sat up and looked at him. "Do I really need to be protected this close?"

"Yes," he said, walking over to stare down at her. "No point in us only doing a half-ass job." She laid there, blinking up at him, trying to process the information. He loved the sleepiness in her eyes. "Speaking of which, if we'll be looking after you, we might as well be really looking after you." And, on that note, he brought her a coffee.

Her eyes widened, and she sat up. "Seriously?" He nodded. She slid off the bed, took the cup from him, walked into the living room, and said, "Careful. I could get used to this."

"Ha," he said, with a smile. "You can't get too used to it."

"Why? You won't stick around?" she asked, as she sat down with her coffee.

"Well, I'm here for a while," he said in a gentle tone.

"But you're not sticking?"

"I work for Levi," he said, "so I'm here. You're the one who's leaving."

"Maybe not," she said, rotating her neck and head, trying to ease the tension in the back of her shoulders.

He saw that she was still pinched up tight, even after the nap. He walked over and gently massaged the back of her neck and the top of her shoulders.

She moaned and said, "How could you tell that was bad?"

"I saw your back and shoulders were tense all the way up." He drew his finger across her shoulder and up the gentle slope of her neck. And then he went back to massaging.

"You don't realize how stressed you are," she muttered, "until you have your shoulders rubbed like this."

"Maybe that's something you should look at, you know? Whether this is the life you want."

"I don't think the stress is from my life as much as it's from the attack," she said.

"In which case we have to end all thoughts of this guy being able to attack you anymore," he said, "just so you can be safe."

"Obviously he's still angry at Levi, so it would be nice if the two of them could sit down and have a talk."

"Well, that would be an ideal scenario, but I suspect this guy just wants to let his guns do the talking."

"I don't understand that propensity for violence," she whispered. "Just the thought of it is enough to scare me."

"With good reason," he said quietly. "But somebody always must counter those who have a natural bent to violence."

"Which is what you do, right?"

"Yes, all of us."

She nodded. "I just like to focus on what is best for the body, like what's the next best medical health discovery or new product," she said, "that can make people happy with themselves."

"And that's great because the world needs that too."

She smiled and looked up at him behind her, as he

dropped his hands off her shoulders. "It's just hard to imagine that the world is so messed up."

"It's messed up, but there are really good pockets in it too," he said. "You always must remember that."

"I guess," she whispered. She handed him his cup of coffee he'd left on the counter and said, "Here, thanks for the neck massage."

"You're welcome," he said, accepting the cup. He looked down at her and asked, "Are you serious about staying in town?"

"Maybe," she said, "it's hard to know what to do anymore."

"You have to follow your heart on some things."

"Following my heart is not a problem, but it's a little hard to sort out business logistics when you're under attack."

"So just park everything until afterward. You obviously trust Levi and Ice."

"I do. We've been friends for a long time, and that helps," she said. "But it's funny how some of this stuff just, well, until you deal with something, you can't even focus on anything else because your mind is constantly drawn back to the one issue."

"And that issue will be gone soon," he said cheerfully.

Chapter 8

"I WISH I had your positive attitude," Dianne whispered.

"Yep," Noah said, "but I understand why you don't. Just hold tight until we can get through this."

"Thank you," she said, with a bright smile. "I wish we could just stay here for dinner."

"We can't?"

"No," she said, "the big dinner tonight at the conference doesn't start till seven." She looked at her watch and said, "Wow, I really slept, didn't I?"

"Well, it's a quarter to six, so we don't have too much time. Is there anything you want to do?"

"Not really, just go over my notes for tonight and tomorrow," she said, "so that I'm prepped and ready to get through each day."

"Well, you've got a handle on that," he said. "So take your time, and we'll go down whenever you're ready."

She went over her notes, drank her coffee, and generally sat and relaxed. Then she got up and did several yoga moves, just to take more kinks out of her body, and, as she did so, he got up and did them beside her.

"It's funny," she said. "I've never really thought of yoga as a group activity."

"It totally is," Noah said. "All around the world people do things like this together. It often motivates more people to do it."

"I guess," she said, "but, for me, it's always been a stress reliever, so I just get up and do it when I need to."

"Maybe you should make it part of your morning routine."

She nodded. "Not a bad idea. Maybe I should try that," she said. "You know what? It's always easy to tell other people how to pick up their lives and fix them," she said. "That's one of the reasons I like these conferences because it helps me motivate myself. I so often see changes that other people have made and the evidence of how well they are doing. So it's one of those cases where you see something that you've let go and now want to get busy and fix it."

"I agree. It's all about motivation, and, once you have the proper motivation for you, then you tend to act on it. The problem is keeping that motivation," he said.

She burst out laughing. "Oh, my gosh, that is precisely the problem," she murmured. It wasn't long before she looked at the time and groaned. "It really is time to go."

"Yep," he said. "Are you good?"

She nodded. "I'll be fine," she said. "I can't say I'm enjoying the conference much because of the extra pressure, but, at the same time, it feels comfortable, and it feels right in many ways because it's what I'm used to."

"A lot to be said for that." He got up as she came out of the bathroom the last time, with her makeup fixed. Smiling, he said, "You look great."

She looked down at the outfit she had changed into. She had put on a beautiful dress that made her feel confident. It was black with a little bit of a white pattern going down one shoulder and across the chest to open as a big flower in her flowing skirt. Dressed in heels as well, she felt stronger and more confident.

He looked at her and whistled. "That's some outfit."

She nodded. "It's not the first time I've worn it," she admitted. "I do like it for classy evening work events, like this."

He opened the door and said, "I like it anytime."

She smiled. "You're just being nice."

"Am I not allowed to be nice?"

"I guess that's part of the question, isn't it?"

He rolled his eyes. "It isn't a complicated question in any way."

"With you, everything's complicated," she said.

"It's not supposed to be," he said, protesting.

"You're a complicated person," she said, "so I find myself checking everything you say."

He stared at her. "Why would you do that?"

She shrugged. "I don't know," she said. "I want to take you at face value, but it's almost like you're too good to be true."

Noah snorted. "I don't know where you got that idea," he said, "because that's not true."

She smiled. "I've met a lot of guys, even some of Levi's crew, but I've never felt that same connection."

"That's not my fault," he said.

"No, it isn't, but it's not mine either."

He shook his head. "This is a stupid conversation," he announced.

"Like many of ours seem to be," she said, as she walked straight down to the elevator and hit the button before he had a chance to.

"I won't make you run down the stairs in heels," he said.

"That's good because I had no intention of doing so,"

she said, laughing.

"He rolled his eyes. "Are you always this difficult?"

"No, are you?"

He groaned. "Okay, how about if we just stop this discussion."

"Perfect," she said, "it's kind of a stupid one anyway."

He nodded. "I just said that."

"That doesn't make it any less true," she said.

"Good Lord, give me strength," he muttered. Another couple got on the elevator at the next stop. They smiled at him, while Noah just nodded his head, studying them from a whole different perspective, but they appeared to be harmless, like hundreds of other people in the hotel right now. It all just made his job that much harder.

When they all exited the elevator at the same time, Di nudged Noah and said, "You really could be nicer."

He stared at her in shock. "I could be what?"

"You know," she said. "You know exactly what you did."

"I didn't do anything," he said.

"Exactly," she said. "You should have been friendlier to them. You could have at least smiled and said hello or something."

"Why would I want to do that?"

"It's called *social niceties*," she said in exasperation. "You really do need to work on your manners."

"No, I don't," he said, glaring at her. "My manners are just fine."

She knew she had gotten to him and, of course, that just made her all the happier. She gave him a cheeky grin as they headed to dinner.

"Says you," he replied, rolling his eyes at her. "You're just trying to throw me off."

"No," she said, "I'm trying to forget." And, with that, she strode quickly toward the back of the dining room, where all the tables were set up. So far, the doors hadn't been opened to let in all the attendees, but that would happen soon enough. As she got up to the front, one of the organizers walked over.

"Everything good?" Di asked.

"Everything's fine," she said. "You're the second speaker of the night."

"Sounds good," Di said. She sat down at her place at the table. The name tag beside her read Noah Wilkerson. She wouldn't get rid of Noah anytime soon. He sat at her side, and, somehow along the line, he had changed clothes too.

"You look very nice, by the way."

"You didn't even notice at first," he said.

She looked over. "Did I hurt your feelings?"

"No," he said in exasperation, "you didn't."

"Okay," she said, "that's good."

"Why is it good?"

"Well, I wouldn't want to deliberately hurt your feelings, at least not in that way. I mean, to bug and to tease you is one thing," she muttered, "but obviously I should have recognized that you had changed your clothes because you recognized that I did."

"No reciprocal compliments, please." He sighed. "Forget it."

She glared at him. "I was trying to apologize."

"No apology needed," he said.

She turned to face him.

A woman from across the table said, "You two are great together. I didn't even realize you had a special partner." Di grinned at the woman. As she went to open her mouth and say something, she got a sharp nudge from Noah, and immediately turned to look at him with a frown.

He just batted his eyes at her. "Oh, we're often like this," he said to the woman. "We just have a little fun with it."

Di winced. "That's true enough," she admitted. "I do take great delight in teasing him."

"That's lovely to see," the woman said, with a smile. "It's funny how different relationships are. But it's always great to have someone you can joke around with and just have fun with."

"Absolutely." Noah nodded.

"How long have you been together?"

At that, Noah jumped in again. "Not too long," he said, "but, when it's right, it's right."

Dianne looked at him, smiled, and said, "Neither of us have done very well in that department in the past," she murmured, "have we, *dear?*"

He gave her a bright smile. "Nope," he said, "we haven't. But that's what makes this so special." She rolled her eyes at him, and he leaned over and kissed her gently on the cheek. "Besides, you're very special."

"Oh, isn't that so sweet," said the woman across from them. "How nice it is to see a couple in love, like you two so obviously are." And, with a bright happy smile, she picked up her glass of red wine, and the discussion turned to the seminar and the speakers for the evening.

Outside of sending Noah a look that spoke volumes, Di could hardly refute the woman's observation.

Dianne was grateful when the evening was finally over because something about his words, the tone of voice, and the look he had sent her, made her rethink her past relationships and made her wonder about the relationship with

Noah that she knew they didn't have, yet now he was confusing her. So was he just a hell of a good actor or was something here? No doubt she really appreciated him being around during this stressful time, and they joked and kibitzed back and forth, which was a lot of fun. He was also looking after her, and this was his job—so it's not like it was a romance. But it got her thinking about how long it had been since she had had one and how strange the concept of a good relationship seemed to be.

She became a little pensive, just thinking about it. She tended to spend a lot of time filling her spare hours and minutes with activities and other people and work, all so that she could substitute this alternative activity for a real relationship. Something that she hadn't given a lot of thought to, but just maybe the whole scenario with being attacked—or maybe just being around Noah—had her rethinking it all. As she stood around this evening, socializing with everybody, Noah came up beside her, with a glass of wine in his hand.

"How you doing?" he asked.

She smiled. "Not too bad."

He wrapped an arm around her shoulders and tucked her up close, she presumed to keep up the appearance and leaned into him quite happily. "You enjoying it?" he asked.

She nodded. "Yes, and no," she said. "I'm tired." With that, she yawned and covered it with a laugh. "Sorry," she whispered. "It's just been a very long day."

"Even though you had a long nap," he teased.

"And I'd forgotten about that," she said, with a shake of her head. "I guess the whole thing's finally catching up to me."

"And that's good," he murmured. "It'll give you a chance to unwind tonight, and then tomorrow morning, you should be ready to tackle it all over again."

She smiled, nodded, and said, "That sounds good to me." She looked around and said, "Can we leave now, do you think?"

"That's what I came over here to ask you," he said, with a smile.

She nodded. "I think I'm ready to go." They turned and walked toward the exit. "I still can't believe nothing's happened."

"That's a good thing," he said. "It's not a waste if we're here the entire week, and nobody comes after you."

"I'm glad you said that," she said. "I have to admit to feeling a little guilty."

He chuckled. "Guilty that you haven't been attacked?"

She shrugged. "I know it sounds foolish, but all of this is in place to keep me safe, and it doesn't look like there's even any hint of a threat."

"Which is when it'll be that much more dangerous," he said quietly.

She nodded and then took several more steps. "Wow," she said, "that last glass really knocked me out."

He slipped the glass from her hand and said, "Come on. Let's get you upstairs."

She took several more steps. "Sorry, I should have called it quits earlier," she said. "I felt a headache coming on a little bit ago."

"It's all right. Let's get you to your room."

She took another step and stopped and, with a funny look, pitched forward.

Noah dropped their glasses and caught her instead. All the time swearing, knowing he should have kept her glass. As soon as he saw her starting to drop, he had put it down but accidentally knocked her glass over. Several other people rushed over. He smiled and said, "She's just really, really tired and tripped." He scooped her up in his arms, snagged her wineglass, and walked quickly out of the room. He had his cell phone in his pocket, but, with her in his arms, it would be hard getting his phone out. He made it to the elevator, pushed the buttons up to the room, propped her up against the side, and pulled out his phone. He immediately sent out a call for help.

As soon as the elevator stopped at their floor, Rory stood outside, waiting for them. He took one look and whistled. "Is she okay?"

"I'm not sure. She passed out. Took a couple steps, said she had a bit of a headache," he said. "Here's her glass. I haven't checked it out."

He snagged the glass and said, "Something white is in the bottom of it."

Grim, Noah nodded. "That's what I was afraid you would say."

"So, even after all that, somebody got a hold of her."

"What we don't know though, is what they slipped her."

"It's not poison?"

"She's unconscious, but she doesn't appear to be foaming at the lips nor has blue extremities nor is having any kind of other reaction, but we need to get her to the hospital fast."

They took her down the service elevator to the basement, where they quickly put her into their vehicle. With Noah holding her in his arms, Rory drove, and they quickly made it to the hospital. They explained what the problem was, and the doctors quickly set about pumping her stomach and checking her vitals. It was an hour before Noah was let back in to see her, still unconscious. He walked over, picked up her hand, and gently held it up against his chest. He looked over at the doctor. "And?"

"It was a date-rape drug," he said quietly.

Noah's eyebrows shot up. "Wow," he said, "that's pretty shitty."

"It is, but it's also a good thing you found her when you did. She was given a heavy dose of it."

"Enough to kill her?"

"No," he said, "I don't think so. Not unless she had some adverse reaction. But it was quite a bit, and she would have been—well, she probably would have just passed out where she was."

"I caught her midair," he said. "She said she had a headache, took a couple steps, and pitched forward on her way to the ground."

"Yeah. But, at that point in time, depending on who was around and who could have helped her, the outcome could have been very different."

Noah nodded at that. "Good point." And none of it bore thinking about because, if it had been any other guy, he might have scooped her up and taken her away. Either way, she'd been attacked yet again, and that made him feel really shitty. "Will she be okay?"

"Absolutely," he said. "We'll keep her overnight for observation, just to make sure the effects of what she did ingest have worn off."

"Okay," he said.

"You brought the glass with you, I heard?"

"Yes," he said, "and I'll contact the police."

"We already have," he said, "and I have a message for you from Levi, which is to stay with her at all times."

"Yeah, definitely," he said, the guilt already rising in him. "I didn't leave her alone in that conference room either though," he said, looking up at the doctor. "But they were handing out wine pretty freely."

"And that's a good delivery system," he said, "especially if she'd already had a drink or two, because she would have been less likely to notice the taste."

"*Great*," he said.

"Listen. As you well know, if somebody is determined to do harm, it's damn hard to get in the way."

"That's true, Doc," he said, "but it still doesn't make me feel any better."

"Well, I'll leave you here," he said. "I can have a cot brought in, if you like."

"Thanks, but no on the cot," he said. "I won't be closing my eyes while she's in here."

"Good enough," he said. "I'll check on her in a couple hours." And, with that, the doctor left.

Noah sank into the visitor's chair, staring down at her. "What the hell," he muttered. "I had my eyes on you the whole time."

And that begged the question of how the drugs got to her, only into her glass? Noah hadn't seen who had passed her that particular glass, and he doubted that she had either. Somebody probably just came along, offered her a glass, and, with that bright smile, she would have accepted it and kept on going. That's how these things worked. Lots of people and nobody watching, except for him. And what kind of a watch was he doing, since he hadn't seen anything either? That would eat away at him. Levi called him just then.

"You're not the guilty one."

"Of course I am," he said in disgust. "You know as well as I do that they managed to get that drug in her hands during that conference."

"Rory said hundreds of people were there."

"Yeah, and I stayed pretty close to her, but we weren't thinking about drugs or weren't considering the thousands of wineglasses being handed out."

"And that's where the problem comes in," he said. "It could have been anybody, and it could have been as simple as somebody specially asking the waiter to give her that glass. The waiter wouldn't have known anything was going on at all."

"No, you're right. She's in here for the night anyway," he said. "The doctor wants to make sure the effects have worn off. It was a pretty-hefty dose that went into her glass too. Rory said powder was at the bottom of the glass, but I didn't think date-rape drugs left a powder."

"No, they don't, but that doesn't mean the powder had anything to do with it either."

"No," he said, "maybe not. Or maybe he just did it so we would be suspicious."

"Maybe. And again, that's just like the attack."

"So we know, but we don't know who."

"Right," Levi said, "the waiting game."

"We're on the cameras all around the hotel," Noah said. "We'll find him."

"Good. Obviously either he's hired somebody else or he's changed his appearance."

"Both probably," Noah said. "And I get the idea this Maxwell guy just wants to hang around, but he's still going after her. Why not Rory or Logan or me?"

"By now he probably will go after you, since he'll know for sure that you're there with her."

"But he doesn't know that I'm your guy," Noah said, "and, if this is all to get back at you, then he'll still target Dianne."

A moment of silence filled the phone. "No, I get it, and you're right," Levi said.

"We need to deflect it from her and onto me," Noah interrupted. "Because now she's been attacked two times—well, three, counting that knock on her head, finding her in her hatch," he said. "I don't want to see a fourth attack. The doctor said it was a heavy dose, and thankfully we got to her fast enough and got her stomach pumped, but, if we hadn't, she would have been out cold very quickly and for a very long time. Anybody could have used that to their advantage." Noah hated to even think about it because just so many damn predators were in this world. Anything like that happening to her just made him sick.

Levi said, "Maybe I should come into town and make myself visible too."

"That's not a bad idea either. It's not her they want. It's you. At least that's the working theory, until we figure out otherwise," Noah said.

"The thing is, he doesn't want to come face-to-face against me. He just wants to hurt those who are in my life, as a way of hurting me," Levi muttered.

"Cowards are like that," Noah said. "But the bottom line is, we have to make sure she doesn't go through this again." When he hung up from Levi, he sent Rory a text, asking if he could bring his laptop and a change of clothes for Noah to the hospital. He was still in his evening wear and would much rather be in jeans and a T-shirt, plus have his laptop.

It wasn't long before Rory strode in with his bag. He stopped and looked down at her. "How is she?"

"She hasn't changed at all," he said. "Still sound asleep."

"But is she asleep?"

"Well, it's a drug-induced sleep," he said. "Not a whole lot we can do about it, until she sleeps through it."

"That's good though. At least, if she's sleeping through it, we don't have to worry about her. She's here, safe and sound."

"Levi said he was looking at coming in."

"Yeah. I'm also a long-term member of the team, so, chances are, if Maxwell sees me around, he might target me as well."

"Well, hopefully," Noah added, "if Maxwell sees me with Levi, he might understand that I'm part of the team too."

"You're the one who rescued her, so there's a good chance he'll suspect that anyway."

"Maybe so. We were trying to pull off the relationship thing during the session tonight."

"And you did damn well with it too," Rory said, with a grin. "You guys look great together."

Noah rolled his eyes at that. "That was for show."

"No, it wasn't," he said. "I watched it. Every time she lifted her head, she was looking to see where you were. You were doing the same."

"Exactly," he said, "that's the job."

Rory shook his head, smiling. "Keep telling yourself that," he said, "but you and I both know that something's going on under the surface between you two."

"Nope," he said. "I like her, yes, but that's as far as it goes."

"No, that's how it starts," he said, "so good on you."

Noah stared at Rory. "Good Lord, you and that whole matchmaking bunch at Levi's are off the deep end."

"Hey, it's fun to see everybody partner up. When you're a happy man, you want to see the rest of the world happy too. Especially your friends."

"Maybe. She does like to bug me," he said. "She teases me all the time."

"That's because she likes you."

"That would be weird," he said.

Rory laughed at that. "Maybe. But whatever works."

"Says you." He just smiled as Rory left. The conversation made him think he wouldn't mind spending some time with Di when this was all over, when they could do it without the craziness that her world was in right now. So far, it wasn't something he could even consider contemplating seriously. Besides, he wasn't sure that she should spend any time with him. He had done a piss-poor job of looking after her so far.

He pulled up his laptop, determined to get to the bottom of something, then immediately asked Levi for access to some of the hotel cameras. Levi gave him links to those inside and outside the main front door. Noah slowly and carefully went through everything. Finding nothing, he asked for more angles from other hotel cameras, and, by the time another four hours had gone by, Noah himself had gone through everything from the parking lot and the front door, yet found nothing.

When he asked for the loading bays, Levi said, "Hang on." A few minutes later, Noah had that link too. Only twenty minutes in, he stopped, picked up the phone, and contacted Levi. "He came in with the caterers."

"You think so?" Levi asked. He quickly brought it to the time frame in question.

Noah said, "That's him there, with the caterers, the fourth guy who just casually walked right past all the caterers in his cooking outfit."

"So, he looks like he's kitchen staff," Levi said, "but the kitchen staff knows that he's not, so assumes he's with the catering crew, and vice versa."

"And he just walked right in," Noah said, alarmed.

"That's quite common in these scenarios with conferences held for a week or a weekend at various hotels. There's no real security, and people come and go. Everybody is trying to do their own job, without worrying about everyone else's job."

"But, in this situation," he said, "that's just bad news."

"Well, it is, but it also makes a lot of sense, during a conference like this, that nobody there in the kitchen is tracking who and what is going on."

"I guess," Noah said, shaking his head. "It'll just make our job that much harder."

"No, not really. We've already got that problem covered," Levi said. "What we need to do is make sure this guy can't access her anymore by diverting his attention elsewhere. So, you stay where you are. We're already heading into town."

"You and Ice?"

"No, me and Stone. He's as identifiable as anyone."

"Meaning this Maxwell guy will recognize him too?"

"If not, Maxwell should recognize me," Levi said. "I mean, to my knowledge, he knew who I was before he approached me on the street, following the death of his child."

Noah thought about the video feed. "Did you notice he stayed in the back? At no time did the cameras pick him up in the middle of the hotel or through the lobby."

"No, and, even through the regular conference events, he keeps a low profile. So, he comes in, and he's got a spot to disappear, then shows up again when he's ready."

"Which just means he hid somewhere until he thought it was appropriate. But he waited to the very end of the evening," Noah muttered. "Why?"

"Everybody's tired. The staff is all busy with cleanup, and she's had several glasses of wine. You guys are more relaxed. Nothing's happening, so Maxwell's got a better, cleaner field to work from."

"Maybe," Noah said. "It will be a long time before I forgive myself for this."

"But remember. You're not to blame."

"Bullshit," he muttered.

"Yep, I hear you. It's always worse when it's somebody we care about."

Noah stiffened at that and frowned into the phone. He didn't say anything because he didn't know what the hell to say. "I'll contact you in a little bit."

"It's what, midnight?"

"Just a little past. Do you really think he's watching?"

"Absolutely. Especially right now, he's looking to see if he's flushed us out or not."

"Then you be damn careful," Noah said, "because he's just waiting for a chance to sabotage you."

"Good," Levi said, his voice hard. "We're just waiting for an opportunity to catch him in the act." And, with that, he hung up.

Chapter 9

I WOKE UP to mostly darkness. A soft light was on in the room around her, and she stared in shock, as she tried to figure out where she was. She studied the walls, shifted slightly, and her gaze landed on Noah, sitting there, poring over a laptop. "Noah?" she whispered.

Immediately he hopped up, set aside the laptop, and took one big step toward her, where he sat down on the edge of the bed. He reached out and gently rubbed his knuckle along her cheek. "How are you doing?"

"I don't know," she said. "My stomach hurts. My chest hurts." She frowned. "My throat—"

"What's the last thing you remember?"

"We were heading up to our suite," she muttered, staring at him with confusion.

"That last drink," he said, "you tossed it back and handed me the glass and said you'd been fighting a bit of a headache for the last few minutes. You were really tired, and it was definitely time to go. So you took a few steps, then pitched forward. I was barely able to catch you in time."

She stared up at him. "Wow. Why?" Her mind tried to process the information, but it wasn't making sense.

"Because you were slipped a date-rape drug," he said quietly.

Her eyes opened immediately, and alarm flooded her

system. "What?" She tried to sit up, but Noah gently pushed her back down.

"You heard me," he said.

She shook her head and then winced. "God," she said, "was it him?"

"Well, I hope so," he said in a joking manner. "Otherwise somebody else is after you."

She just stared at him and sank deeper into the bed.

"That's gross," she said. "I didn't even notice any difference in the taste."

"And that's partly why he waited so late in the evening. You would have had a few drinks, so less aware. It is tasteless, colorless, odorless, all that good stuff."

"It's a perfect drug then, isn't it?"

"For predators, yes," he said. "And that just makes it all that much harder to deal with."

"Sucks though." She stared around at the room. "So, he didn't get me, and I'm not hurt?"

"He didn't get you, and, no, you're not hurt. I carried you out of there, told everybody you just tripped, and Rory met me in the garage, and we brought you here to get your stomach pumped."

"Jesus," she said, "I guess that's why my stomach hurts."

"Absolutely," he said, with a smile. "So, besides your stomach, how are you feeling?"

"Well, my head hurts," she said, "and my throat feels thick. Even my voice feels wrong."

"To a certain extent it is, but that'll all get better as you recover."

"How long am I staying here?"

"The doctor wanted you here at least overnight, just to make sure you've worked your way through the drugs in your system."

She sighed. "You mean, pumping my stomach didn't get it all out?"

"I think he just wanted to make sure that he didn't let you go, if there was any chance of you having a relapse."

"I get that," she said, snuggling deeper. "And I have to admit that I'm still quite tired." Even as she said that, she yawned.

"Okay," he said, "it's still very early. Just go back to sleep."

She stared up at him, as he returned to his seat. "You'll stay here?"

"Absolutely," he said.

"You're not to blame, you know?"

"Several people have tried to tell me that."

"And I suppose you don't believe them, right?"

His gaze was dark, filled with guilt of course. "I was the one there looking after you," he said. "Obviously I did a shitty job."

"No," she said, "that doesn't wash for me. You got me out of there before anything more could happen."

"But you're the one who was affected."

"I was," she said. "The stupid thing is, I wasn't even going to have any more wine. I was done."

"So why did you?"

"The guy who handed it to me said the glass was from you."

He stared at her for a long moment, then nodded. "I guess that would make sense," he said.

"For him, yes," she said, "and, of course, I didn't think anything of it. I just thought it was a nice thing for you to do."

"Like there wasn't enough wine flowing?"

She nodded, with a smile. "Didn't even think of that, did I?" She shook her head. "Just goes to show you how gullible we are."

"We are gullible because we think the best of people," he said. "The problem is, nobody thinks beyond the fact that it's a great evening and that you're all having fun. It's all good, so you don't see or even want to see the darkness in other people."

"I know I certainly didn't," she said. "I didn't question it for a moment."

"Which made it easy for him," he said. "He used my name. You were tired, and it was the end of a long evening. You'd already had what? One glass? Two glasses?"

"I don't even know," she said. "Enough that I'd decided I was done."

"Now, if only you had followed through on that," he said, with a smile.

"If only." She nodded. She struggled underneath the sheet, and he quickly unpacked the blanket on the foot of her bed and pulled it up over her shoulders.

"Thank you," she said. He leaned down and gave her a gentle kiss on her temple. She smiled. "Why do I suddenly feel like a two-year-old?"

"Well, you're injured," he said. "I can hardly kiss you any other way, can I?"

"Oh, but you want to, do you?"

He snorted.

"Right, part of the act and all?"

"Hell no," he said. "You're a beautiful woman. Of course I'd be happy to kiss you."

She smiled. "I wonder how much of that is an act too?"

And then she dozed off.

"NONE OF IT," Noah said quietly into the darkness. "Not one bit." And he didn't even know what to do about that. All he knew was that he didn't want to leave her side, wanting to stay close to her all the time. It was a hell of a job he had going on here. He was supposed to stay close to her, and that was the good thing. But he was also supposed to keep her safe, and that part he'd not done a very good job on. He understood why everybody was trying to let him off the hook, but honestly he didn't want to be. He wanted to catch this asshole and to make him pay for hurting her.

Three times now.

He couldn't believe that. It seemed so stupid to use somebody like her to hurt Levi. Noah understood that Dianne was first a friend of Ice's and then a friend of Levi's, and it wasn't a business thing, so, of course, it increased the pain when somebody hurt a friend to get back at you. You wanted them to come after you, but that would have been too fair of a fight. This Maxwell guy clearly wasn't into fair fights. He was into taking advantage and hurting people.

Noah just wished this guy would come after him, but Maxwell wouldn't be that strong. He would take his time and toy with them some more. Sitting back down, Noah was determined to go back to the camera footage and discover where this guy had slipped out of the hotel. There had to be a way to track him and to find out where he was staying. But, so far, none of their efforts had produced solid leads.

Every time they were left fighting to see who exactly was going after them. Or who they were chasing. They didn't know who the culprit was in this case. They had photos of him, but why the hell was he always slipping away? Noah settled back down for more work on the videos, finding Maxwell had gone into the hotel—looking like himself and quite happy to be caught on the camera apparently—but had left looking like someone completely different.

Finally Noah pulled a profile pic and caught the nose and the set of his shoulders. He sent it to Ice, who confirmed Noah's gut.

She called him. "That's a hell of a disguise he's using on the way out."

"That's why it took us so long," he said, yawning. "Bastard."

"But," she said, "we've tracked him to a small vehicle on the road now."

"Good," he said. "Can you track him to a house or wherever he's staying?"

"That's the plan," she said. "But he's likely using a fictitious name and could be anywhere."

Chapter 10

WHEN DIANNE WOKE the second time, Noah stood at the window, staring outside, his hands in his pockets, a pensive look on his face. She studied his profile and whispered, "Now that is a lovely picture to wake up to," she murmured.

He immediately walked over to her bed. "What was that?"

Her smile kicked up the corner of her lips, as she said, "You heard me."

He chuckled. "I notice you say that when you're hurt and injured and lying in the hospital bed."

"Meaning, if I had said it in my own bed, it would change the outcome?" she asked, her eyes widening in interest.

He tilted his head, raised his eyebrows. "You're playing with fire."

"I don't have a problem with that," she said. "Do you?" She looked at him with interest. "You look like the kind of guy who can take charge and handle whatever is thrown his way."

"I'd like to think so," he said, smiling down at her. "But definitely not with injured women."

"Hey, I'm not injured anymore," she murmured. "I was just supposed to stay long enough for them to check and make sure I'm okay."

"And how are you feeling?" he asked.

She nodded. "Much better," she said. And just then she yawned, a big expansive yawn. She stretched her arms up over her head and said, "There's still a weird kind of flatness in my brain as if, you know, something's not quite right. But I'm feeling pretty decent."

"Good," he said. "Do you think you can get up and go to the bathroom by yourself?"

"I need to," she said, "but—"

He asked, "Do you want me to get a nurse for you?"

"Maybe, I'm not sure if I'm ready yet." She laid there on the bed, staring around the room.

"Are you okay to go back to the conference?"

She wrinkled up her face at that. "I need to. Today's not very involved for me, so that's good," she said. "If it was a repeat of yesterday, I don't think I could have done it."

"What do you have to do today?"

"This afternoon, from two to four, I'm doing a workshop," she said, "and then I'm done."

"Good," he said, "maybe we can get you through that."

"That's what I'm hoping," she said, shifting. "Then, once the conference is over, I want to go back to Levi and Ice's."

"They would really like to have you there. If nothing else it will lure Maxwell toward them."

"I'm surprised they haven't come to town."

"Oh, Levi's already here with Stone," he said. "And we've been hunting this guy all night. We actually found him coming in the hotel and leaving again many hours later on the camera records. So, he found a place somewhere in the hotel to hide."

"If you think about it, he could have just rented a room in some other name to have a place to disappear to, then show up when he needs to do the deed. He may have even been planning on grabbing me himself at that point in time."

"It's quite possible," he said. "Luckily I came up to you right then."

"I remember," she said. "I had the glass. I took a drink, and then you were there."

"Which is a good thing," he said, "because otherwise he might have picked you up and moved you out himself."

She shook her head. "I'm not going down that pathway," she said. "That will give me nightmares for a lifetime."

"You and me both."

She reached up, grabbed his hand, and said, "Remember. This is not your fault." He looked down at her, and she saw that he had absolutely no intention of forgiving himself. She sighed. "Hey, any chance of coffee around here?"

"That might be possible," he said. Then, checking his watch, he shrugged and said, "Well, maybe not. It's still pretty early."

"I'm sure, with all your amazing resources, you can get me a coffee," she said in a wheedling tone.

He chuckled. "Always the child."

"Nope," she said, "nothing childlike about me at all." And then she batted her eyes at him. "If you give me a chance, you'll find out."

"What do you mean, *give you a chance?*" he protested, with a smile. "We haven't even gotten that far."

"That's because you're slow."

Immediately his jaw dropped, but the door opened, and a nurse walked in. He swallowed whatever retort he had ready, as Dianne looked over at the nurse and smiled. "I'm feeling much better. Can I leave now?"

"Not so fast," the nurse said, with a smile, "but it's great to hear you're feeling better." She explained to Noah, "I need to do a full checkup of Dianne, and we'll get her to the bathroom to see how she is for walking."

"Okay." And, with that, Noah was ushered outside, without much chance to argue.

Di looked over at the nurse. "You must have a well-honed technique in order to get that to happen."

The nurse laughed. "Absolutely," she said, "and he looks like one who could make life a little bit difficult."

"You think?" she said, laughing. "He is quite the character."

"You are a lucky lady," she said. "He obviously cares deeply for you."

Di didn't have anything to say to that, wondering how everybody else saw the two of them. The fact that it was just a business thing still irked her because she wanted it to be something that was so much more and thought she saw that he did too. But she would have to deal with it when she was finally out of here. Soon the nurse was finished and, after a successful trip to the bathroom and back, said, "I'll bring the doctor back in a few minutes."

"Oh, good," she said, "I was afraid he wouldn't show up for a couple more hours."

"No, he's been here all night, and I know he's likely to head home soon, so let me see if I can grab him." And, with that, she took off.

Di settled back against the pillows, wishing she had coffee or that she'd remembered to ask the nurse for it.

Noah stepped back inside, something hot and steamy in his hand.

She looked at it, at him, and said, "That better be coffee, and it better be for me." Her tone was so flat, and her delivery so perfect, when he looked at her, she chuckled. "Ha. Fooled you."

He sighed. "It is for you," he said.

"And I was just regretting not having asked the nurse for coffee, but, if she brings the doctor back, that would be even better."

"Yeah, that would be great," he said. "Then we could get you out of here."

"That would be divine." As it was, she hadn't even finished the coffee when the doctor showed up.

A few minutes later, he said, "Yep, you're good to go." And he promptly left.

She smiled up at Noah. "Now that's good news." She looked at her clothing, her evening wear, hung on a hanger nearby, and groaned. "I should have asked you to bring me something."

"Not an issue," Noah said. "We'll go straight back to the hotel, and you can either go to bed or have a shower and change there."

She winced, as she started to get up. He stepped outside of her room, so she could get changed, but she drew the line at her shoes. Putting on heels when she felt like shit was a little bit more than she could handle, so she picked them up in her hand, and, still wearing the hospital's no-slip bootie socks that they'd given her to wear, she walked out to the hallway, to see him standing there, talking on his phone.

As soon as he saw her, he hung up, turned to look at her, studying her carefully top to bottom. When he got to the footwear, his lips twitched.

"I don't think I can stomach putting heels on right

now," she said quietly.

"You don't have to," he said. "Walk out with your head up. Absolutely not a problem."

She snorted. "I can do that," she said. "Just watch me." Then she proceeded to stride confidently and surely out of the hospital—in her blue hospital booties.

⁂

DAMN, NOAH LIKED Dianne's confidence. And her style. He was still chuckling when he led her to the vehicle and then helped her get into the front seat. She put her high heels on the floor and said, "Am I ever glad to get out of there."

"I'm sure you are," he said. "It was still the right place for you last night."

She wrinkled up her nose at him. "Are you sure?"

"Positive," he said, "and I really hope you don't do that to me again."

Her eyes widened. "Oh, right, I did this to you," she muttered. He chuckled. As she relaxed back, she said, "Man, I just want to go back to my place."

"And what place is that?"

She stopped, thought about it, and said, "Good point. Home hasn't been home for a very long time."

"And what about your hotel?"

"Well, I'm happy to be going to the hotel right now," she said, "and I'll be even happier when we can go to Ice and Levi's."

"That sounds good to me too," he muttered. "Yet we can't forget about the fact that this was the third attack while you've been here."

"No, and I don't know if this was more dangerous or

not."

"Well, we don't know the intent behind his actions," he said. "Was he there watching and just planning on having you collapse and get rushed to hospital, or was he planning on whisking you away?" He watched a wince slip across her features, and he nodded. "Not what we want."

"Hell no," she said. "That's nothing I want at all."

"On the other hand," he said, "now that we have you back again, and we didn't see any sign of this person at the cocktail party last night, I have to wonder just what he had planned."

"Maybe it just hit me all that much faster than normal," she murmured.

"And I was considering that too. Maybe you would have made your way up to the hotel room, not feeling great, and he would have picked you up there."

"That's what I was thinking too," she muttered. "But I don't plan on having any drinks with anybody I don't know really well for a long time."

"That's one of those lessons that you don't let go of easily, isn't it?"

"Absolutely." He drove her back to the hotel. As she got out, she stared down at her feet and sighed. "Okay, it was one thing to walk out of the hospital like this," she said, "but it's another thing entirely to walk through the lobby and head up to my room." Quickly she pulled off the hospital socks and slipped on her heels, only wincing slightly.

He smiled at her but deliberately refrained from making any comment. He held out his arm, and she slipped her own through it.

"You know what it looks like."

"It looks like you had a very nice night," he said.

She snorted at that. "Of course it does. However, I don't care what other people think," she said, holding her head high. They walked through the lobby to the elevator, then moved on up to her room. By the time she was inside, she crossed over into her room and threw herself down on the bed.

"Do you want to sleep some more?"

"No," she said, "but I'll have a shower and a coffee." She groaned as she got back up again and found a pair of leggings, a long tunic, and some underclothes. "If you can handle ordering the coffee," she said, "I'll grab a shower." And, with that, she headed into the bathroom.

She heard him on the phone before she started the water but wasn't sure who he was talking to. It really didn't matter; she desperately needed a shower. Under the water, she just stood there for a long moment, letting the heat soak into her skin, feeling her body strengthen, as it finally relaxed. When she was dressed again, she stepped back out, a towel wrapped around her head.

He looked up, smiled, and said, "You look about eighteen."

"I don't know if that's a compliment or not," she said good-naturedly. "That's definitely younger than I was going for. But you didn't say forty, so that's good." He laughed. Just then came a knock on the door. She jumped, then frowned, as she watched him walk to the door.

He looked over at her reassuringly. "Coffee, remember?" She nodded slowly but didn't move. He opened the door and let a trolley be pushed inside. He tipped the waiter, shut the door behind him as he left, and then brought the trolley to the couch. "Come and have something," he said.

"I guess that means we aren't going out at all today."

"You tell me," he said. "Did you need to go shopping or something?"

"I don't know," she said. "I don't really feel like shopping." She had to admit that she was still feeling pretty drawn and tired. She walked over, sat down on the single big chair, then watched as he poured two cups of coffee. She accepted hers with a smile and set it on the coffee table beside her. "Food though," she said, "is another story."

"I didn't think you would want hospital food," he said.

She winced. "Hell no, that's not on the menu. So, if you want, we could head down for the convention lunch that's a few hours away. I think I'll probably be fine," she said. "I can wait until then."

"Unless you wanted to put in an appearance somewhere along the line. You said your workshop was from two to four, right?"

"Yes," she said, "but still it's pretty normal to put some time and effort into all the conference activities."

"Got it," he said. "So, if you're up for it, we'll have our coffee here. Then, once you've got your hair the way you want it and all, we may go down and visit for a bit at the conference, like an hour or so before lunch, then eat there, and afterward come back up here again. Gives you a chance for a short nap before you give your workshop."

"That sounds like a plan," she muttered. "Did you find anything out about who it was who drugged me?"

"We can only assume it's the same guy," he said, "but I didn't see him on the hotel cameras after the fact, outside of leaving the building. I only wish I knew what his plan had been."

"Me too," she muttered, "or maybe I don't."

"It's always better to know," he said, "at least in my

book. It lets you deal with whatever the issue is, even if it's bad."

Very quickly, she felt edgy, like she needed to go downstairs. By the time their coffee was gone, she had curled her hair into a bun at the back of her neck, had freshly applied her makeup, and she was ready to go.

He looked at her outfit and grinned.

"It's casual but funky," she said, with a shrug.

"I like it," he announced. Then he hopped up and escorted her to the door.

"Is it okay down here, do you think?" she asked, her steps faltering, as she made it to the doorway.

His arm immediately came around her, and he said, "Yes, it's safe."

She looked up at him with worry. "I know you say that, but—"

"I'm so sorry about last night," he said. "So our lesson right now is, *don't eat or drink anything.*"

"Aren't we going down for lunch?" she asked humorously.

He smiled at that. "It's a buffet, where you can pick and choose yourself, and we deem that safer than a catered affair delivered by waiters because we don't think Maxwell will hurt hundreds of others just to get to you."

"I agree. I don't think that's the intent," she said. "Otherwise it would have been easy enough to just bomb the hotel."

He looked at her askance. "God forbid," he said.

She winced. "I wasn't suggesting that Maxwell would do that. I was just thinking that it was something that he could do if it wasn't just about targeting people close to Levi."

"Exactly."

Downstairs, she found herself looking around more and more. "It's so weird," she said to Noah. "Now I'm looking at everybody."

"And yet it's all about him," he said. "We saw him on the cameras last night."

"So how is it possible," she said, "that he was even allowed to come in?"

"Levi's already contacted the catering company to confirm, but, from the looks of it, Maxwell just walked in with the true catering crew. With so many people working at the same event, yet for different companies, they didn't know who he was, yet nobody cared, figuring he worked for the other company. He used a disguise when he left."

"It's just a comedy of errors."

"Not so much that as it exposes a weakness within the system. The fact that, if somebody does want to get at another person, it's damn easy to access sites like these to do it."

She shook her head. "And I thought tight security was everywhere in a hotel."

"No," he said, "not at all."

"The things you find out the hard way."

Downstairs in the lobby, several people greeted her normally, reinforcing the idea that nobody really knew what had happened. When she was handed a cup of coffee, Noah deftly removed it from her hand and said, "I'll go get you one myself."

She looked at him with relief. "Thanks," she said. "I really could use more."

Noah found one of the big urns, with a lineup of about ten people there already, when one of the kitchen staff brought out another big one. The line split into two, and

Noah stood in one of the lines and got a cup of coffee for her. Carrying it back, he studied the area and heard Rory in his earpiece say, "Glad to see you guys here."

"She's feeling better, but now she's pretty nervous."

"Understood," Rory said. "It had to be a shock to find out how easy one can be set up for an attack like that."

"I think that realization, plus the fact that she didn't see it coming, has her on edge."

"You too, I hear?"

"I was right there with her, and she was still taken down," he said. "How do you think I feel?"

"I don't think you can take that one on yourself," he said. "It's pretty hard to keep drinks from being spiked in a setup like this. He only needed a second to make it happen."

"If we can't keep something like that from happening," he said, "what the hell will I do about coffee and lunch?"

"We've been watching the caterers all day," he said, "and we have guards posted in the kitchen to keep track of people coming and going."

"Do they know what happened?"

"I spoke with the head chef. He's pretty upset about the whole thing," he said. "The catering company is one that they've used a lot, and the chef certainly doesn't want anybody tampering with his food, so he's pretty adamant about keeping security on it."

"Well, that's something," Noah said. "I doubt Maxwell will try the same thing again, and I highly doubt he'd risk injuring five-hundred-plus people by tampering with the food, but we can't take that chance."

"Right," Rory said. "I think the next time he'll be a little more hands-on again. It didn't work to do it from a distance, and now either he will attack her or he'll come after one of us."

"Well, let it be one of us," Noah said, as he reached her and handed over a cup of coffee.

She looked up, catching his words. "Are you talking to Rory?" He nodded. "How is he?" she asked warmly.

Rory chuckled in Noah's earpiece. "See? That's Di. She always thinks about everybody else before herself."

"I know," Noah said. He smiled down at Di. "Rory is doing just fine. Everybody's keeping track of the food to make sure there isn't a repeat of last night."

"Good," she said. "I don't think Maxwell would be so foolish anyway. Wouldn't it be more likely in the chaos when everybody's checking out?"

"Not a bad idea," Noah said, with a nod. "Enough people will be coming and going that it would be easy to lose him in the crowd again."

"But we won't be leaving at the same time, right?" she asked, searching Noah's face.

He nodded. "Exactly."

The late-morning convention activities progressed calmly, as she socialized and visited with various vendors and clients. By the time lunch was served, Noah sat down beside her and barely ate. His gaze was too busy on everyone else.

She reached over and patted his hand. "You can eat, you know."

"Not hungry," he said.

"That bean salad is awesome."

"It might be," he said, "but, if I'm not hungry, I don't eat."

"Yes, but, in your job, you should be eating," she said, "because you need the fuel regardless."

"I'm far more concerned about keeping an eye out

around here."

"I understand," she said. She took another bite and munched away at it. "It all seems so harmless here, ... until something happens. It's like realizing a serpent's in heaven or something. It all looks so perfect on the outside, only to find evil underneath."

"That's a good word for it," he said.

"I'm not religious," she said, "but you certainly realize, once you've been attacked, that there's an element to life that you don't deal with normally. One that's much darker, much deeper, much more unpleasant than anything else you've ever faced before. I don't like it."

"It's the underbelly of society," he said, murmuring close to her ear. Just then another friend walked over and grinned at her.

She leaned down to Di and whispered, "He's gorgeous," and then she bounced away.

Dianne turned a wide grin to Noah.

He flushed at that. "I hope that wasn't about me."

"It absolutely was," she said in delight, then cast him a sideways glance. "And she's right. You are absolutely gorgeous."

He felt the heat flushing over his face.

She chuckled. "Hey, you may as well just own it," she said.

He gave a shrug and tossed her a grimace. He never had been very good at accepting compliments. This was a fairly personal one. He didn't say anything.

"You handled that well," she whispered a little later.

"What?" he said, hoping she would just drop it.

"Well," she said, "a lot of people don't know how to accept a compliment."

"I don't think men get very many of them," he said, "to put it bluntly." She thought about it and then nodded slowly. "You know what? You could be right. Women tend to expect it, but I'm not sure they hand them out very much."

"It's kind of a double standard."

"But life shouldn't be like that," she said seriously. "Everybody should give credit where credit is due."

"My looks are hardly something to take credit for."

"Maybe not," she said, "but your smile is and the kindness in your eyes. The physical fitness that you work so hard to achieve certainly is."

He looked at her. "My eyes are kind?"

She chuckled. "Yep, they are, indeed."

"Well, I guess that's one thing then," he said, with a smile.

"It is," she said. She looked around at the table. "How about a walk outside?" He frowned at that. She looked up and said, "Just a little one, for some fresh air, and a chance to get out a little bit."

"I think there's a rooftop deck," he suggested.

She looked at him in delight. "Is there? I had no idea. Oh, yes. They had construction going on up there last year."

"I think so," he said. "Come on. Let's go check it out." They got up, made their excuses and goodbyes, and walked over to the front reception desk, where he asked about it. And, sure enough, they had finally finished the rooftop garden over the last year. Following their instructions, the two headed up.

As she stepped out into the fresh air, she gasped. "Oh, my gosh, this is lovely up here."

A running track circled all the way around on the perimeter but, on the inside, were flowers, green plants, various trees, and benches. He had to admit he was impressed. "This is a nice space," he said. "I can see, during the craziness of a convention like this, with workshops and such, it would be great to get away for a few minutes, when the schedule allowed. This would be a great place to do it."

"Absolutely," she said, filled with surprise and delight, as she wandered around. "It feels so natural and so fresh."

"Well, I think the sunny day helps too," he said in a dry tone.

She looked over at him, smiled, and said, "Okay, I'll give you points for that one too."

"Wow, I'm winning today," he said in a mocking tone.

She rolled her eyes at him. "Now I'll have to take a point away for all the sarcasm."

He burst out laughing at that, and she grinned back. He really loved the natural ease that existed between them. Just like the way the comments rolled back and forth to one another. He would never take offense at anything she would say, knowing she would never mean it in a bad way. If she made any kind of comment, she almost always followed it up with something nice. At her core she was a good-hearted person, and those were the kind who often were mistreated in this world. It was too bad but a fact of life.

After walking through the running path because it was deserted, they sat down on one of the benches in the center, and she tilted her face up to the sky.

"We only have about an hour," he warned.

"I'll take it," she said quietly. "It's just so peaceful up here."

"I'm surprised more people aren't up here," he murmured, as he looked around. Unfortunately it was also a hell of a good place for an attack. Like an ambush, where nobody was likely to see you.

"Don't even start thinking about all that nasty stuff," she warned.

"You mean the nasty stuff that keeps you safe?"

She laughed. "Yeah," she said, "and, as long as you're thinking about it, I guess I don't have to. So go ahead, keep thinking."

"You're very ... innocent," he murmured.

"Hell no, I'm not," she said, opening her eyes in astonishment. "I don't think that's the term you mean."

"Naive?"

"No," she said. "I'm not naive either."

"So, what are you?"

"Honest," she said, "or does it not come across that way?"

He thought about it and then realized she was correct. "No, you're right," he said. "I guess that does suit you pretty well."

"See? I mean, if it's something good, I tell you," she said. "If it's something bad, I tell you."

"But I can't always tell if you're joking or not."

"Well then, you should ask," she said, "because I'll tell you then too."

"Maybe it just means that it wasn't funny," he said, tilting his head sideways at her, "if I can't tell."

She smiled. "Okay, fine," she said. "I'll give you that one too."

He chuckled. "Am I winning yet?"

"Hell no," she said, "no way."

He just grinned and settled into his seat. "It is really nice here."

"I'm seriously surprised," she said. "I've been here over the years, and I didn't know about it."

"It wasn't ready. They've only finished it this last year."

"Right, that makes sense." She looked around and said, "There's something about the atmosphere in broad daylight like this, where you never think of anything nasty happening, but look at that cloud." She pointed up to the sky. The cloud was big, dark, and looked like it was swollen with rain. "If that were to close over the sun, it would immediately change the atmosphere and make this a spooky, scary place to be, and I'd start looking around every corner."

"The trouble with that is," he said, "then you start expecting good things on sunny days, and you aren't looking for the bad things."

"Well, I'm never looking for the bad things," she said, "but I get what you mean."

"I guess what I'm saying is that bad things happen in broad daylight too."

"Too often I guess, yeah," she said, "but it's all about atmosphere, don't you think?"

"Maybe," he said, with a noncommittal shrug. "While you're sitting here enjoying it, I'm looking at how deserted and empty it is, wondering if our guy has any idea this is here."

"I'm sure he does," she said, looking at him, "because he would be the kind to check out every entrance and exit."

"And every hidey-hole. For all we know, he was up here hiding yesterday."

"I'm sure you can check the cameras."

"Maybe," he said. "That isn't a bad idea." He pulled out his phone, and, while she sat and relaxed, Noah contacted Levi to see if any cameras were up on the rooftop deck, specifically to see if their perp was up here last night, while they knew he was in the building but couldn't find him. He sent several photos of the place to show Levi what it looked like and how there were lots of places to hide.

With that done, he put his phone down and turned to look at her. She had her eyes closed, and she was just resting, with her head back. "You want to go back to the room and lie down?"

"No, I don't," she said instantly. "I'm just really enjoying being up here."

"It looks like you are falling asleep," he joked.

"Nope, I'm not," she said, with a bright smile. "I'm just relaxed, and that's something that's worth a lot to me."

"Of course."

A couple employees appeared with huge wicker baskets and garden shears and cut many flowers from the gardens here. Noah gave them a smile and a short nod. They left shortly thereafter. Noah's phone rang a little bit later. "What did you find?" he asked Levi.

"You're right. That's where he was."

"Okay then," he murmured, as he straightened up, looking around. "Do you have the same cameras or any way of checking now to see where he might be or if he's around?" He didn't want to mention Maxwell's name and make it too clear because Di was just sitting here, relaxing.

"Yeah, I just did a sweep," Levi said. "Just the two of you."

"That's good to know," he said, trying to keep the relief out of his voice.

"Don't let her out of your sight," Levi warned.

"No, we just have to get through today."

"And tonight," he said.

"Yeah, I was wondering about heading to your place a

little earlier than planned."

"If she's up for it, we are," Levi said. "Talk it over with her, and see what you want to do."

When Noah hung up the phone, he looked over at Di, staring at him with a puzzled look. "What?"

"You never mentioned anything about going to his place early."

"No, but it seemed like something we could consider."

"I am supposed to be at the conference tonight," she admitted slowly.

"I know. That's why I hadn't brought it up," he said, "but you also have to be here tomorrow morning, I thought."

"Not necessarily," she said. "It's just the end of the workshops, and there'll be a couple speeches, but I'm not giving one."

"So, in theory, you could leave early?"

"I could," she said, nodding. "And you know what? That would be a nice idea. Get through tonight, and we could go to Levi's tomorrow."

"Which is what we were planning anyway."

"Yes," she said, then frowned. "We could, of course, go a little earlier and just leave tonight."

"That's up to you."

"Given what happened last night, I'm leaning toward that, now that you brought it up," she admitted.

"Good," he said. "I'll follow through on whatever you want. You just tell me."

She grinned. "I do like a man willing to make things happen."

He laughed. "Particularly when it comes to your safety."

Her smile fell away at that, and she nodded. "I guess that's what it's all about, isn't it?"

Chapter 11

DIANNE WASN'T SURE why any time Noah brought up his operation, it made her feel sad.

"Don't even go there," he warned.

"Too late," she said, with a wave of her hand. "I'm already there."

"Then get off of it."

"Not so easy to do," she snapped back.

"Well, that's a good start," he said. "Find that temper of yours and make things happen the way you want them to happen."

"It's not quite that easy," she said.

"Sure, it is," he said. "Just don't get hung up on all the negatives here."

Knowing that he didn't quite understand what her problem was, she just kept quiet. Finally she looked down at her watch and said, "Unfortunately it's time to go."

"We can come back up later, if you want. If we're staying here for the evening, we could even come back up and watch the city lights."

She nodded in delight. "Now that, I am definitely up for. It would be beautifully romantic." He looked at her sharply, and she smiled up at him. "If you have any romance in your soul, that is." He immediately started protesting. She laughed and said, "I'll race you to the stairs." And she beat him.

She didn't know if he let her win or not, but she did win, and that kept a smile on her face, as she headed into the workshop for the next session. The next few hours were crazy busy, and, by the time she was done, she looked up at him and said, "Wow, I could really use a trip back up to that roof."

"Let's go," he said immediately.

She thought about it and said, "Let's take up a coffee."

"Maybe you should just have water or something," he said. "Seems like you're running on coffee."

"I always run on coffee," she said, with a shrug. "It's not even the caffeine. It's more that it's my comfort drink."

"Sure," he said doubtfully.

She glared at him. "You're not taking away my coffee."

He held up his hands in mock protest. "No, I'd never do that." He added an eye roll.

"Ha," she said. "Now you're just mocking me."

"No," he said, "it's probably too early for you to have a glass of wine up there, so coffee it is."

"Or a pot of tea," she said, wondering.

"Well, that would be something different for you."

"I really like my tea too. I just rarely order it when I'm out though."

"Why is that?" he asked, as they wandered back to the front reception area.

"Mostly because it's hard to get a good cup, when you're out." He burst out laughing at that. She stared at him and said, "It's not that funny, you know."

His laughter stopped, and he looked at her in amazement. "Seriously?"

"Absolutely," she said, and then her smile twinkled up at

him.

"You're joking," he said, shaking his head, "and I fell for it."

"No, not so much joking," she said, "but I do find that tea tastes different when I'm out."

"Just because it's different doesn't mean it's bad though," he said.

"No, it doesn't mean it's bad at all, but different is different."

He nodded at that. "So, what'll it be?" There was almost a dare in his tone.

As they walked toward the little coffee shop, she said, "Maybe we'll try tea then." Instead of a teapot, they ordered tea in a big takeout cup. She left the tea bag inside, but he brought up a little bag for the garbage. "Aren't garbage cans up there?"

"I'm sure there are some," he said. "I doubt the hotel can afford to not have them everywhere."

"I get that," she said. "Everybody is being more conscious of things like that these days."

"I'm sure they try to set a standard, but it's very hard to follow through. If they put garbage cans out there in a public space, somebody has to remember to empty them. Because the minute they aren't emptied, somebody will complain, write a nasty review about the cleanliness of the place."

"I didn't even think of that," she said, "but you're right. People will be people."

"You've got to consider that too, if you are seriously considering buying a natural food franchise."

"It's all about reviews and customer satisfaction," she said, with a nod.

"And do you want to be tied down to something like

that?"

"Well, I would hire staff of course," she said. "I wouldn't necessarily have to work it myself all the time."

"I guess it depends on how successful you expect it to be."

"Very successful of course," she said, "otherwise I wouldn't do it."

"But you still have to put in a certain amount of work."

"Yes," she said, "but then, if I don't, what else would I do? This is the work I do." Together they walked upstairs, carrying their hot cups. "I'm still amazed at this place," she said, as she stepped out onto the rooftop garden.

"Imagine what it will be like in a few hours," he murmured.

She nodded, her smile wide. "Maybe we can come back after the evening session too. I want to take advantage of this beautiful place as many times as we can, before we leave this hotel."

"That's fine," he said, "but I won't be leaving your side tonight, and you won't be drinking anything that I'm not vetting."

"Good," she said. "I was a little worried about that."

"Don't be," he said. "We can't guarantee that all the food is safe and that somebody isn't out there trying to tamper with it," he said. "All I can do is guarantee that they won't get to you."

"And you can't even guarantee that," she said, turning toward him. "You can't keep taking all of this on yourself."

"I can and I will." She rolled her eyes at him. He just smiled, and they sat down on a bench in the same place they were before.

"So, nobody's seen him since, huh?"

"No," he said, "the problem is, once he left here, he could have gone to another hotel. He could have gone to his vehicle. He could have gone home. He could have been any place where the cameras wouldn't have picked him up."

"And, of course, he was disguised at one point for sure, so it didn't really matter where he went."

"Exactly, but we're now looking for that disguise, for his true face, and anything in between," he murmured.

She sighed. "It still feels like he's out there, and he's got the upper hand."

"He does. We're on defense, and that's always a much harder position to defend," he said. "Much better that we take the offensive position and know exactly where this guy is, so we can pick him up, but that just isn't where we're at right now."

"No," she said.

"Are you okay to stay here tonight?"

"I think we should," she said. "We're safe at the moment. He's likely to keep trying, but we've already paid for the room."

"The room expense is minor," he said. "If you want to leave, we certainly can."

"No, I think I'd like to be here for this evening," she said. "I'll have that talk with somebody who's here about a franchise."

"Good enough," he said. "We have a couple hours yet anyway," he said, "so why don't we put down our tea and walk."

She laughed and said, "Good point." Putting their cups down, he walked her over to the running path, and, because it was still empty, they quickly did four laps.

When she sat back down again, she was slightly out of

breath. "Wow, it's not—I don't know if it's because I'm out of shape," she said, "or because I was drugged, but that took more out of me than I like to admit."

"It doesn't take long to get out of shape," he said. "But it's also pretty easy to pick it back up, particularly if you're in good shape to begin with."

"Well, I don't know how good a shape I am in after being here and seeing everybody again. Seeing everyone always inspires me, but, at the same time, it can be very depressing."

"That inspiration is what you should take from here," he said. "It's much easier to handle."

"It is, but that doesn't make it any easier when you're looking at the difference between where you want to be and where you are."

"And that's why the whole process of change is so painful for so many people," he murmured.

"I often wondered if I should be doing classes."

"Taking them or giving them?"

She burst out laughing at that. "Both," she said. "It's always a matter of looking at what you have to offer, then also looking at the things that you want to build up strength in."

"When you get settled," he murmured, "all kinds of things can happen. But maybe you should give yourself a chance to get through this stressful period of your life first. Get moved, get the franchise, and let yourself get settled in for a few months, before you decide what you still might need to learn."

"Is it normal to feel so insecure when you're contemplating something like this?"

"Well, if it's new and different, of course," he murmured. "Think about it. It takes you out of your comfort zone, and anything that does that is stressful, which is the number one dream killer in the world. So you need to work at getting that stress level down."

"Yes, boss," she said in a cheeky voice.

He chuckled. "See? That's what I like about you," he said. "We can talk. I can say anything to you that I need to say, and you don't take offense."

"I don't have time for taking offense," she said.

"Neither do I." And they stayed here for the next couple hours, until it was time for dinner. With another look at his watch, he said, "I'm sorry, but it's time to go."

She nodded. "I knew it," she said. "I was trying to hang out for a little bit longer."

"Do you need to change before we go?"

She looked down at her outfit, shook her head, and said, "No, I'll go to dinner like this. Then I'll probably change it up for the evening."

"Good enough," he said. He stood up and reached out a hand.

She didn't even think about it and placed her hand into his and let him lead her back down toward dinner.

◦◦◦

NOAH STAYED CLOSE through dinner, and he stayed close through the evening speeches and then the entertainment afterward. It was now mostly a cocktails-and-mingling atmosphere. As the evening went on, he saw that her energy was wearing down. At just after nine, he walked up, slid an arm around her shoulders, and pulled her closer. "So, are you ready to head up?"

She looked up at him gratefully. "Honestly," she said in a low tone, "I was ready to leave half an hour ago."

"Too bad you didn't say something then." She walked over and said goodbye to several people, who were still there, since she wouldn't see them again. He looked over at her as they walked out. "So, how did your meeting about the franchise go?" He'd stayed nearby during that meeting but had deliberately blocked out the conversation.

"I think it went well," she said. "We're ready to set the lawyers to work on it again."

"Good enough," he said.

"Not that it's really an issue for you," she said. "Hopefully all this will be well and truly dealt with before then."

"It might be an issue if I decide to take you—invite you—on a date, when this is all settled."

She looked up at him. "And you know what? I just might say yes."

"You think?" he said. "I'd hate to go in that direction if you're aren't sure."

She reached up and patted his cheek. "I'm pretty certain it's a safe bet."

"Well, maybe not though," he said. He led her through to the elevators and up.

"It hasn't felt the same tonight," she said, with a big yawn.

"No, it hasn't," he said. "I'm still trying to figure out what's going on."

"But you're expecting something?"

"Definitely. I'm not exactly sure what or how, but it still feels like trouble's brewing."

"It does feel like that, but it didn't seem that way at the reception tonight." And he agreed with her. "On the other hand," she said, "that could just mean that way more is going on that I'm not prepared for."

"Maybe," he said. "But we'll see where it goes."

"Right," she murmured. Back at the room, she stepped in and walked to her bed and kicked off her heels.

"So now what?" he said. "Are you ready to sleep?"

"Hell no," she said, "I want to go upstairs to the rooftop deck with a glass of wine, so we can sit and enjoy the lights."

He laughed at that. "Ah, right back to being romantic."

"Hey, you're the one who just mentioned a date."

"I did, indeed," he said, "but this is hardly a date."

"No way, you're not getting off so easy on that," she said. "That's a cop-out."

"Not a cop-out," he protested.

"Well, let's just say it doesn't qualify as a true date."

"I just said that," he said in exasperation.

"And I was just agreeing with you," she said, batting her lashes at him.

He shook his head. "You'll make me crazy."

"That's okay," she said. "I'm already crazy being around you." With the kibitzing still ongoing, he led the two of them back upstairs to the rooftop deck. As soon as he opened the door, he could tell he'd made a mistake.

But she was already pushing her way behind him, chattering away. And then she stopped and gasped.

"Oh, my God, what happened here?"

Chapter 12

DIANNE STARED IN shock at the flowers that had been decapitated all across the beautiful rooftop deck.

"Well," Noah said in a quiet voice, pulling her back up against the door, as he assessed their surroundings, "I'll say we had a visitor."

"This could have been a kid though, right?"

"It could have been," he said, with a quick nod. "I'm not sure why they would do it though."

"Because they're kids," she said succinctly. "You turn your gaze away for a moment, and, next thing you know, they've decapitated the flowers."

"Maybe," he said, but he didn't sound convinced.

She looked up at him. "Do you really think this is something Maxwell would do? It's very unfocused and not directed at me."

"Unless he was listening in and heard us say that we were coming back here."

She frowned at that. "I really don't want to think that he was listening in."

"No, but we can't toss out that possibility."

"Maybe not," she said. "Can we go into the garden, do you think?"

"I'm not sure we should." He stood at the door, weighing the odds.

"Well, if someone just had a temper tantrum with the flowers," she said, "I would still love to sit and look at the lights."

"Let me call security first," he said.

She sighed. "Fine," she said, "you do you."

He studied her, as he made the call. "The manager is on his way up," he said, when he ended the call.

"Good." But he was already on the phone again. "Now who are you calling?"

"Levi, to see if he has anything on camera."

"Oh, right," she said. "That's a good idea."

But when Levi checked, he said, "The cameras are down."

"Well, I'll take that as a yes then."

Just then the manager stepped out onto the deck and gasped in horror. "Oh my," he said, "after all the effort we went to. We really wanted to make this perfect."

"Exactly," she said. "I still want to go see the gardens, but Noah is not very thrilled."

The manager shook his head, as he walked forward.

She could almost hear tears in his voice and realized this was a personal project of his. "I'm so sorry," she called out.

He stopped and looked back at her. "Did you have anything to do with this?"

She immediately shook her head. "No, of course not. I love this space."

He just nodded and kept looking. He walked all the way around the perimeter, then came back. "It's all of them," he said, his tone heavy. "Every one of the flowers."

"Why, though?" she asked. He just shrugged and looked very sad. She wanted to apologize again, but, since he had already misconstrued her words, she didn't think it was the smartest thing to do.

Noah looked at the manager. "Do you have cameras out here? Maybe you could check and see what and who did this."

He looked at him, smiled. "I do, indeed," he said. "Let me go check." Before he left, the manager looked over at her. "I'm sorry, but I don't think you should be here right now."

She frowned at him, looked at the flowers, then back at Noah. He was nodding. Her shoulders sagged.

The manager ushered them off the rooftop and headed to the stairs. They followed. He looked at them and said, "Are you coming this way?"

Noah nodded. "Yes, we like to take the stairs when we can."

"Good, good," he said. "I'll go check security." And he raced down the steps.

Noah turned to Di. "Well, do you want to go for a walk instead? We can sit out in the back of the hotel in the atrium. They also have a rooftop garden as well," he said.

She shrugged. "Let's just go back to our room."

As they headed back to the room, they met two other people from the conference and were invited for drinks in the bar. She hesitated, then looked over at him. He just waited for her to make a decision. Finally she thanked the couple and declined. "I'll just go back to my room to get some rest," she said. And, with that, she continued toward her suite.

"Is that really what you want to do?"

"Well, I kept thinking that, if someone decapitated all those flowers as a warning to me," she said, "I didn't want to be around anybody else and get them hurt."

"That's really a smart way to think of it," he said, and

she felt the intensity of his gaze. "I know this is hard on you. But, even when the chips are down, you're still thinking of others."

"Usually I do. It's harder now, looking for Maxwell everywhere," she said.

As they reached the suite, Noah grabbed her hand. He put a finger against his lips and pointed, and she stared, seeing that the door was ever-so-slightly ajar. She looked up at Noah, who just shook his head. He waited, tucked her up against the wall, and gently pushed open the door.

She heard no sounds inside as he did so, and she wasn't sure what he was expecting. If somebody had broken in, chances were they were long gone, and, if they had a visitor in there now, she didn't know if he would jump out and attack them right at the doorway or not. All she knew was that she wasn't budging. Noah sent a message to somebody by reaching out and pressing something in his ear; he must still be connected to Rory.

At that, she looked around, wondering if the other men would appear. Sure enough, a few minutes later, while they stood silently at the doorway, Rory showed up. Then the two men—one high, one low—went inside and did a quick search, while she stood in the hallway. They came back almost immediately and ushered her inside. As soon as she stepped inside, she stopped and cried out in shock, "Why? Why all the destruction?"

"Another message," Noah said quietly.

"Well, I'm getting damn tired of the messages," she snapped. "And the cryptic nature of it. He might be pissed at Levi, but he doesn't need to keep hassling me like this."

"Well, I suggest we make the transfer tonight, unless you have a problem with that."

"What do you mean?" she asked, as she turned to look at him.

"If you still want to stay here overnight, we'll have to change rooms," he said. "The other option is that we go straight to Levi's tonight."

"Let's go to Levi's tonight," she said immediately.

He nodded. "And I have to get the manager back up here as well."

"Oh, great," she said, sagging down onto the couch, which had only one cushion left. "He'll probably blame me for this too."

"I don't think he blamed you for the flowers," he said, quietly explaining to Rory what happened. "I don't think he blamed you. I think he was every bit as shocked and upset by it as we were."

"That's true," she said. "He was obviously very involved in the creation of that garden and was heartbroken at the devastation."

"And nothing that you saw there pointed to anything?" Rory asked.

"I phoned the manager and stayed with her, instead of looking around," Noah said, "but I wish I had."

"Well, you stay here with Di," Rory said. "I'll go up and take a look." With that, he quickly disappeared.

The manager wasn't long in arriving, and, when he saw the room, he was just as upset as he was about the flower garden. He kept making comments about it, looking at them suspiciously, after yet another incident of destruction of property.

Finally she turned to him and said, "I can't stay here another night," she said, her tone stiff. "Your hotel is obviously not safe. The security is dismal."

He looked at her in shock, then immediately offered excuses and assistance in getting her another room.

"No," she said, "I can't do that. I've stayed at this hotel chain in various cities over a lot of years," she said, "and this is the first time I've had such trouble."

"That's not fair," he said. "We've never had this kind of problem before."

"Maybe not before," she said, "but you definitely have a problem now." She held her ground, and, looking at Noah, she said, "Let's move to Levi's tonight."

He nodded and said, "I'll make that happen."

⁓

NOAH MADE IT happen all right. By the time Rory returned from the rooftop deck, his face grim, they were packed up and checking out. She would get a credit for the one night, and the settlement to be done for the damage to her personal items would be handled soon. She couldn't even tell if anything was missing in all this mess.

Noah looked over at her. "Maybe you can give them an itemized list tomorrow."

She nodded and looked at the manager. "I really am very upset about this whole thing," she said, "and I need to leave."

"That's fine. I understand," he said. "Contact us tomorrow, and we'll discuss taking care of your losses."

She nodded. As they walked down toward the lower level, where the vehicle was parked, she asked Rory, "What did you find upstairs on the roof?"

"What makes you think I found anything?" he said in a cagey voice.

She snorted. "It was pretty evident from the look on

your face."

"Just a message for Levi."

She groaned. "And we didn't see it, right?"

"No."

"What was the message?"

"*I'm coming for you.*"

"But," Dianne said, "Levi wasn't mentioned by name?"

Rory and Noah shared a look.

"Is Levi still in town?" she asked them.

"He was this whole evening," Rory said. "He was at your workshop."

She stared at him in shock. "You're kidding. I didn't even see him," she said.

"He was visible but invisible."

"Jesus, if I didn't see him, what are the chances that Maxwell did?"

"Oh, I think Maxwell saw Levi," Noah said, Rory nodding. "Levi didn't stay all that long. He just put in an appearance, then Stone came to wander around."

"So, Maxwell should know Levi and Stone are here," Dianne said. "So the message was about me, not Levi? So Maxwell is still coming after me?"

"That's a message in itself," Noah said. "Basically saying, he can do what he wants, whenever he wants to do it."

"That's pretty arrogant," she said.

"Yep. So now we move the fight to Levi's compound."

"And are any of Levi's people still in town Maxwell can come after?"

"Several of them, but it won't be you."

From the look on her face, she was sure Noah could read her expression—that she both hated and loved that answer. "I know it's wrong of me," she said, "but I'm really happy to hear that."

"It's not wrong of you at all," Rory exclaimed. "We don't want you to deal with any more of this."

"And I don't want to deal with any more of it either," she said. "It's just that this guy is so focused on hurting Levi that he doesn't care what method he uses."

"These guys seeking revenge are like that," Rory said quietly. "They focus on one thing and one thing only, and everything else is collateral damage."

"Well, I don't consider myself collateral damage to anybody," she said in a hard voice. "I still keep thinking of it over and over in my mind, wishing I had done something different or found a way to get back at him. I just—it's still something I'll have to deal with."

"Exactly why we'll move you to Levi's now," Noah said. "You've finished up what you needed to do for the conference, so now we'll get you back there again."

Rory drove, with Noah sitting in the front passenger seat, as she sat in the back.

"Is there a reason why I'm in the back seat?" she asked in a conversational tone.

"Yes," Noah said, before Rory had a chance to explain.

"Okay, and what's that reason?"

"I'm keeping an eye on the vehicle following us."

She froze.

"And," he said, "don't look now."

"As soon as you say that," she said in a furious whisper, "all I can think about is turning around."

"I know," he said, "but that doesn't mean I want you to."

"Dammit," she said, "you can't just say something like that to somebody. You know what it's like."

"I do know what it's like," he said in a cheerful voice.

Rory laughed. "I wouldn't worry about him," he said to her. "Noah likes to tease."

"I've noticed. He does way too much of it," she announced.

"Ha," Rory said. "You're just as bad."

She thought about it and then said, "Okay, maybe you're right there."

Rory chuckled. "Glad to see you two are getting along so well."

Noah rolled his eyes at that. "Don't go there, man."

"Definitely don't go there," she warned.

"Why is that?" Rory asked, looking at her through the rearview mirror.

She groaned. "Because he's already asked me out on a date."

"Well, that's a good thing, isn't it? Or maybe not. Maybe you turned him down, and he's struggling with rejection."

"Ha. I doubt he ever gets rejected," she said.

"I do too," Noah said, turning to look at her. He studied her to see a worried look in her eyes. Immediately his attitude softened. "Hey, it'll be okay."

She sagged and looked up at him, and he caught a sheen of tears in her eyes.

"I'm sorry," he said. "We were really hoping to keep this ugliness away from you."

"I think that's one of the problems in life," she said. "The more you try to keep somebody from seeing the ugliness, the more the ugliness overwhelms the world, and you have no way to avoid it."

"I don't think it's quite that bad," he said, "but we'll be home soon."

"Except for the fact that whoever is following us is probably coming home with us too."

She'd sunk down low enough that her head didn't show above the seat. "Are you trying to hide?"

"What if he's got a gun?" she countered.

"Good point," he said. "Glad to see you keeping your head."

"Not only am I keeping it," she said, "I want to make sure I'm keeping all of it."

He blinked at that for a few minutes and then grinned at her. "Got it. Listen. If you want to lie down sideways, we've still got another twenty minutes, if not longer, before we get home."

"Fine," she muttered and stretched out sideways.

As soon as they hit the long stretch of the more deserted highway about fifteen minutes from the small town outside the compound, a single shot was fired. Noah barely even heard it, but the tire blew almost immediately. The vehicle fishtailed from side to side. He immediately looked for the following vehicle but saw no sign of it. Behind him on the back seat, Di struggled to even stay on the seat. "Are you okay?" he asked her, as Rory got control of the vehicle.

"I will be," she said, as the big truck slowed and rolled to a stop on the side of the road. "I guess we didn't expect that to happen."

"It's not so much expected, but you have to be prepared for the unexpected," he said. "We've already radioed to the compound, and we have help coming."

She nodded slowly. "But that doesn't mean it'll be in time."

Just then, a second shot rang out, and, hitting the driver's window, it bounced off.

She stared at him.

"Remember? That's why we took this vehicle. Bulletproof glass."

She took a long slow deep breath. "You could have told me that before I laid down back here."

"No," he said, "it made you feel that much safer."

She nodded. "It did, but, if I'd realized it was bulletproof glass, it would have felt that much safer still."

"I told you earlier." He shrugged. "I didn't know if you believed me."

"No," she said, "I just didn't remember."

"Well, we just reminded you again."

She groaned. "Are you always this difficult?"

"Are you?"

At that, Rory was chuckling again, even as he pulled a handgun from the glove box. "Do we have anything longer?"

"Not here," Noah said, "coming though."

"Good," he said. "What about you?"

"Just a handgun."

"But," Dianne added, "Ice can fly her chopper here faster than anybody can drive here." She got excited at that prospect.

Noah and Rory both shook their heads. "The sniper can hear the chopper long before it shows up, and so he'll be on the move."

"And then we're just waiting? Is that all we'll do?"

"Nope," Rory said. "Ice has other toys, like a drone if needed. But remember, we are also hooked up to satellite feeds, so she and Stone will track down the shooter and will relay that to the guys on the ground. In the meantime, I'll get out and disappear into the woods, track this guy on foot."

"There are no woods," she said franticly. "News flash, there're no woods in this area."

He looked at her, grinned, and said, "No, that's very true," he said, "but there are lots of shadows." And, with that, he disappeared.

She stared after him. "Why didn't the shooter shoot him?"

"The only time he could have got him was when the door opened. Beyond that, Rory is incredibly stealthy."

"And we're now just sitting ducks."

"Well, the vehicle is locked, and we're inside bulletproof glass, and we have help coming."

She kept shaking her head. "That's not good enough."

"What would you like to do?"

"I'd like to leave," she said, her voice serious and low.

He looked at her and said, "Where would you like to go?"

"Out of the vehicle."

He thought about it and said, "Okay, we can do that. Some taller grass is over there, if you want. We won't hide very much though."

"No," she said, "like I want to be out of the way, out of sight, and safe."

"I got it," he said, "but we are seriously in the best position we can be in out here in this stretch of flat ground."

"Not if he's got something bigger than a handgun or a rifle," she whispered.

He looked at her, and she was dead serious, probably thinking of her all-too-recent attack in that rental car. "We can leave," he said, "and I can take you into the shadows and keep you safe, if that'll make you feel better."

She immediately nodded. "It really would," she said.

"I'm starting to panic in here. It feels like a coffin, not a safe place."

"Okay," he said. "I'll come around to get you on this side of the vehicle, since the last shot hit the driver's side." He quickly unlocked the front door and then added, "Now I want you to stay as low as you can, and we'll run up behind that little rise over there. The shot came from the far side, but we can't be sure he's still there. So get ready." At her silent nod, he slipped out on his side, closing the door quietly, none of the interior lights turning on with the door opening, and he pulled her out of the back seat. He whispered, "Three, two, go." And the two of them raced, bent over, as fast as they could, until they came to the small hillock, where they both threw themselves to the ground.

He cursed softly.

"What is it?" she asked.

"Lost my Bluetooth."

"Uh-oh. You're not connected to Rory any longer?"

"Nope. Gotta wing it for now."

She lay here gasping, rolled over onto her back. "I don't know if leaving the truck and running here was a stupid thing or a smart thing to do."

"Well, it'll be a fifty-fifty decision," he said, "depending on what's happening now."

"Yet you let me make that decision. Why?"

"Because I felt uneasy too," he said. "Instinct was telling me to run, and sometimes you just have to listen to that." As they sat here together, staring up at the stars, the silence around them was eerie.

"It feels ..." And then she couldn't even get the words out.

"I know." He reached across, grabbed her fingers, and

said, "Just hang on. We have help coming. Remember that."

"I know," she said. "I just have that horrible sense that something's about to happen."

Boom! The vehicle exploded right in front of them. She went to sit up, but he pushed his arm across her chest and held her down.

"You need to say down, especially right now," he said. "That's likely to bring all kinds of people here, and they'll be looking for movement."

"Unless they think we're still in the vehicle."

"We want the bad guys to think we're in the vehicle. So let's not do anything to show them that we're not."

She sank back down. "What if we were still inside?" she cried out softly.

He rolled over, held her close, and said, "But we weren't."

She stared at him blankly. "But we were," she said.

"And we left. We followed our instincts. We left, and we're fine."

She blinked several times and then she burst into gentle tears, as he held her close in his arms.

"I promise. It'll be okay."

She shook her head. "Oh, my God," she said, "how can you promise anything?"

"You're still alive, aren't you?"

At that, she leaned back, looked up at him, and said, "Yes," she said, "I am. But, God, it seems like it's getting closer each time."

His face was grim, when he nodded. "I hear you," he said. "But remember, we're still fine."

In the distance he heard vehicles. "And now the cavalry has arrived."

"Thank God," she whispered. "But where's Rory? I'm worried about him."

That's the one thing Noah wasn't worried about. Rory was a big boy, and he'd been doing this a hell of a long time. "He's fine," Noah said. "Don't you worry about Rory. We just need to make sure that the new arrivals don't get shot too."

She stared at him, and the tears leaked even more.

He wished he had stayed quiet about that last part.

Chapter 13

VERY QUICKLY, DIANNE was engulfed with Levi's crew. She was helped into a vehicle and spirited away. She twisted to look behind her, but she saw no sign of Noah and asked Logan, "Is it safe to leave him behind?"

Logan looked at her in confusion, then realized she was talking about Noah. "Not only is it safe to leave him behind, it'll be a fight to get him to leave. He wants to find this guy and get payback. Same with Rory and the rest of us."

"Ah," she said, settling back into her seat. "I can understand that. I wouldn't mind a chance to punch him myself."

He grinned at her. "The fighting spirit, we like that."

"Not much fighting has been done at this point," she said. "All we're doing is evasive maneuvers."

"That's exactly right, and now we need to take that up a notch."

"But we can't do it unless it's safe."

"I like the way you think."

She shrugged. "I'm not even sure I'm thinking straight anymore," she said. "It's just been attack after attack after attack."

"And they're escalating," he said, with a nod. "I'm sure you realize that."

"I do," she said quietly.

"And obviously it's a huge concern. But you're not

alone, and we're here to help."

"I'm glad to hear that. After that conference this week," she said," I was really looking forward to a chance to unwind."

"And you can unwind as soon as you get to Levi's."

She looked over at him and, after a moment, asked, "Can I really though?"

He smiled. "Nobody'll get to you in the compound."

"No, but I can't stay there forever. Ice isn't running a hotel."

"Maybe you should mention it," he said. "You never know. She might be totally okay doing just that for you."

She laughed. "I don't think so. She's got chaos happening with her own family now."

"Not chaos as much as craziness. But that goes along with having kids."

"Anybody else pregnant?"

"Not any who are talking," he said, "but I have my suspicions."

She looked at him. "Really?"

He shrugged. "Well, once Ice and Levi got married, others followed suit. When she got pregnant, you know it was only a matter of time."

"Right. It's like she put a stamp of approval on both."

Logan chuckled. "That's one way to look at it. I don't think Levi would stop it, no matter what."

"Do you think he wanted to?"

"Nope, I don't think so. I just don't think he thought it was the safest choice, considering the industry and all."

"But Ice spent all that time and money to make the compound safe."

"Exactly."

With that, she realized that he had neatly turned the conversation around on her. She sighed. "Okay, okay," she said. "I get it. If Ice thinks it's safe enough for her children, chances are, I'll be fine."

"You'll be fine, while you de-stress, decompress, and relax."

"Pretty sure those three words mean exactly the same thing," she announced.

"So, in that case, you should have gotten the message three times over," he said, with a smile. And just then, they took the turn toward the long driveway leading to the compound. She looked at the huge space and said, "She's really done a hell of a job."

"They both have," he said, with a nod. "Not everybody lives right here, but we all come back and forth on a regular basis."

"It's like a huge family, isn't it?"

"It is, and one I wasn't sure could work long-term, but," he said, "I've been more than pleasantly surprised. Something is very special about being part of a group like this, where there's mutual respect, understanding, and acceptance."

She nodded. "And love, apparently."

"Absolutely," he said. "Love is a huge part of it. Not just for each other but for the families we've brought in. The extended families are working out beautifully."

As they neared the compound, the gates opened for them, and she smiled. "Everything's under lock and key, right?"

"Even more so right now because of the attacks," he said. "Nobody's getting in here who isn't allowed to be here."

She took a long slow breath, as she sat up taller to see Ice standing out front, her hands on her hips, as she studied the layout ahead of her. "She's always on watch, isn't she?"

"She's always a warrior," Logan said quietly. "A hard lesson learned, and one mantle she'll never put down."

"How sad that she has to be so vigilant."

"It's the work she does. Work that both of them chose. This isn't a job that's nine-to-five, and then it's over on the weekends or on holidays or even after your twenty years. This is a lifetime career. She knows it. Levi knows it, and they'll do everything they can to not only protect themselves but everybody they help in the world."

She sighed. "And here I am, thinking about opening up a natural food franchise in town. It sounds completely boring and useless compared to the work she does."

He burst out laughing. "And you know she'd have a lot to say about that too."

She chuckled. "That she would." And, with that, she hopped out of the vehicle and walked up to Ice, who opened her arms, and the two women hugged.

"Oh, I'm so sorry," Ice cried out, "this is just going from bad to worse."

"The truck blowing up was pretty rough," she said, "and it wasn't even mine."

Ice burst out laughing. "There's a reason we have high insurance premiums," she said. "Don't you worry about the vehicle."

"Hey, it was bulletproof but not bombproof?"

"Probably a rocket launcher," she said comfortably. "Although I didn't hear a loud woosh."

Di just stared at her and shook her head. "I know it's Texas, and we're allowed guns, but, jeez, when is it okay to carry that kind of stuff around?"

"Happens all the time," Ice said, with a shrug.

"Scary though," Di added.

"It can be, yes."

"And you're still okay to be in this industry?"

"Somebody needs to do it," she said, with a sideways look at her.

"I know, but that could be somebody else too." Dianne didn't know why she was persisting, but it just seemed hard to understand why Ice would continue to work in a field like this, even though it was so dangerous, especially now that she had Hunter.

"Not only does somebody have to do it but somebody has to organize the fight against evil. Somebody has to keep everything safe, and somebody has to keep normality happening," Ice said.

"That's the trick, isn't it? That normality part? Half the world functions in a way that nobody else really realizes. How messed up is it that most people go about their daily lives clueless, while you handle a lot of these shadowy cases that people are better off not knowing about."

"That's why keeping the base normal is so important," she said, "because it's not just the stress of our business, but it's also the health and safety of all the people who work for us. We need to make sure that they're whole and healthy and happy too."

"That's a lot to take on."

"It is," Ice said, with a gentle smile. "But I think I'm pretty good at it."

NOAH KNEW IN his gut that Levi and his men were conducting an organized search of the hills. Noah had been out fifteen minutes, maybe twenty, and had covered just one mile, as he studied and looked out into the darkness. He thought he'd seen something up in this corner and was moving his way toward the spot, but he hadn't seen anything move since then. As he sat here in the silence, listening, a rock tumbled off to his left. He immediately crouched lower to the ground, as he studied that area. And then it came again.

He smiled. Since he only heard one rock disturbed at a time, that was a good indicator that it wasn't an animal moving about. Since they moved with four legs, it generally caused more rocks to shift. He waited and listened, smiling as the sounds came closer and closer.

There was a chance this wasn't the shooter Noah was looking for, but he'd bet it was. As he waited, he heard another footstep. And another.

Then it stopped.

Noah studied the darkness ahead of him, and *there*. He vaguely confirmed the outline of a man standing. He had a weapon over his shoulder, a handgun on his hip, but he was turned slightly away from Noah, so it was hard to make out who it was. Noah didn't recognize him as one of the team, but the man was just unclear enough that Noah couldn't risk making a mistake. Then the guy turned and headed toward him, directly to the spot where Noah hid. He watched him take two more steps and then stop, as if filled with that inner knowledge that something was wrong in his world.

Of course what was wrong was Noah. He would make sure this asshole knew it too.

Almost as if he just realized the danger he was in, the man turned and bolted to the right. Noah leaped off the ground, like a jackrabbit, running as fast as he could behind the gunman, but the ground was almost shale-like here and tumbling under his feet. The only good thing was that this guy had the same problem. The shooter gained the trees just ahead of Noah, who burst through into the brush, hitting the ground, knowing the guy would be turning with his gun in his hand, ready to take him out.

No shots were fired.

Noah waited, listening ever-so-quietly, his own gun up. Now this was a case of the stealthy rabbit and the hunter after his prey, and Noah just had to make sure he was the one who came out on top. As he listened, he thought he heard an odd birdcall. He didn't dare answer it, but it could be one of Levi's team. It was a call they used regularly. But, if they were coming in his direction, they were just as likely to get themselves shot too because this guy was hunting anybody and looking for a target, any target. As long as it was connected to Levi, this gunman would chalk it up as being a good shot.

Just as Noah thought it couldn't get any worse, he heard a second birdcall. He knew the search was heading in his direction. He hadn't checked in, and now they were coming to see if he was okay too. An almost imperceptible sound—the clearing of a throat—could be heard, maybe ten yards away. Noah shifted silently, so he had a better view. Then focusing on the shadows ahead, he waited for the man to show himself. And slowly, ever-so-slowly, his prey stood and lined up his rifle to take a shot.

Immediately Noah jumped to his feet, hoping to alert his team. "Hands up," Noah snapped. The man froze, but he didn't drop the weapon. "Lower your weapon," Noah ordered, "or I'll shoot."

The gunman gave a broken laugh. "I don't give a shit if

you do shoot," he said.

"You've been targeting Levi," he said, "and that poor woman in town."

"She's nothing but one of Levi's whores," he said. "She should know better than to lie down with the devil." None of that even made sense to Noah. "I don't know who you think she is, but she has nothing to do with Levi."

At that, the man stiffened. "Everyone to do with Levi is walking with the devil," he said. "The man could have done so much, and instead he chose the wrong side."

"He's not to blame for the death of your child."

"My son," he snapped. "It was my only son."

"Levi's still not to blame," Noah said, swearing in his head for not being more specific.

"You don't know anything about it."

"I know you asked for help and that he wasn't in a position to give it."

"He could have. He just didn't make it a priority."

"He was doing another job in the States and didn't have any men free to go to Australia. Was he supposed to stop and let everybody else suffer because you were suffering and needed saving too?"

"I didn't need saving," the man said in a vindictive voice. "My son did. I'd have done anything to save my son."

"And yet you couldn't. That happened, and it's unfortunate," he said, "but you need to accept it. It wasn't your fault, and it wasn't Levi's fault." He knew that other people moved in the darkness around them, so he had to keep this guy talking, keep him focused on Noah. He also needed to get that damn gun away from him. "You didn't have to go after Di."

"Why not?" he said. "They were friends. I figured it

would be a way to get at him. Slowly picking them off, one by one."

"How many have you killed?"

"One," he said, "but Levi didn't even know, making it completely useless as a method to hurt him."

"Who was it?"

"Roger, someone Levi knows out of Sydney, but I guess the relationship was too distant to cause him to even notice," he said. "I fixed his vehicle so it went off a cliff. Levi didn't even know." There was a broken laugh, as he shouted, "He didn't even fucking know. Somebody lost his life, and Levi didn't even care."

"It's not that he didn't care. He didn't know, like you just said," Noah replied. "You know he cares."

"I hope so," he said. "I hate to think all that effort I put out was in vain."

And that was part of the bottom line here too. It wasn't about the victim at all. It was about the effort *he* went to, to create what he wanted out of this.

"So, you killed a man, and you're only worried about the fact that you may have wasted your time and effort, instead of the fact that you might have taken a man's life uselessly?"

"I'm sure he had a good reason to die. Everybody's a sinner."

"Including yourself."

"Absolutely," he said, "including myself."

"So maybe you're to blame for your son's death."

At that, there was a moment's silence. "I'll kill you for saying that," he said in a way-too-quiet voice.

"Maybe," Noah said. "But you're pretty busy blaming everybody else and taking lives, making innocent victims out of people who had nothing to do with the death of your son.

Is that how your son should know who you are? Do you think he's not up there, watching you?"

"I hope he is," he cried out passionately. "I want him to know that I'm avenging him. I want him to know that I'm doing everything I can to make up for this."

"You mean, everything *now* because you couldn't do it back then."

"That's not fair," he cried out. "He wasn't supposed to get hurt."

At that weird wording, Noah asked, "What do you mean, wasn't *supposed* to? Did you have something to do with his kidnapping?"

"It was an insurance scam," he said, "but it went wrong, and they decided to take it to a whole new level. I needed Levi to go after them."

"There are other teams in this world that do the same work Levi does."

"But he should have done this for me."

"Why is that?" Noah asked curiously.

"Because it was his idea that I do the insurance scam."

Noah knew that was a lie, another twisted scenario that this guy had concocted to relieve himself of guilt. "No way," he said flatly. "That isn't true. This was your own messed-up deal. You just decided to lay the blame on Levi to make it easier on yourself. You needed a target, and Levi happened to be a good one. But he isn't an easy one."

"But he's not a hard one," the gunman said. "He's nothing but a pumped-up arrogant asshole."

"You should know something about that," he said quietly.

"And you, you're nothing but a dog in heat, chasing after that bitch."

"Yet you're the one who gave her a date-rape drug," Noah said, ignoring the words meant to anger him, to distract him. "The woman doesn't have anything to do with you, and you're busy hunting her down, attacking her at every corner."

"Of course. Mostly just as a lesson to prove that I can and that you can't stop me. That Levi and his circle will never be safe."

"Nice," he said, "and yet here I am, with a gun on you."

"So," he said, "I've still got a gun in my hand. I'll take you out, and you can do your best to take me out," he said, "but I'll survive with a handgun. You won't survive this at all."

"Maybe not," he said, "but I'm quite happy to die trying. At least I know that I didn't kill any innocents in this world to ease my own guilt for not having been there for my child."

At that, the man roared and shot randomly in Noah's direction.

Only Noah wasn't there.

Chapter 14

D I COULD TELL from the odd look on Ice's face that something was going on. They had been sitting here, having a cup of coffee in the dining room, at a huge long table that offered comfort, peace, and family gatherings. Alfred hovered to make sure Dianne was okay and kept patting her hand, telling her to relax. But, as she watched Ice, Dianne saw something cross her features. "What's the matter?" she asked urgently.

Ice refocused her gaze back to the conversation. "They found him," she said quietly.

"And is it over?"

"No," she said, "a shoot-out is happening."

"Oh, crap," she said, staring at Ice in horror. "Noah's in danger?"

Alfred squeezed her fingers and said, "Calm down. These guys know what they're doing."

She stared at him blindly. "But it's Noah."

"It is Noah," he said, his gaze searching hers.

She blinked at him. "What if he's hurt?"

"If he's hurt, then we'll do everything we can to get him back on his feet," he said quietly. "It happens. But that doesn't mean it's got to be fatal."

She took a long slow deep breath. "No," she said, "of course not." But she felt herself hyperventilating, and her world was spinning. "I'm not usually this affected," she said, "but it's been a hell of a crazy few days."

"Of course," he said quietly. "Plus, somebody you really care about is involved."

At that, she refocused on his face and stared. "Did I say that?"

"You didn't have to," he said.

"Well, he's been looking after me this week."

"Sure he has."

Alfred was thinking something completely different. Then again, maybe she was too. "I'm so confused," she whispered, as she sagged in the chair, her gaze going from his face to Ice's. It was obvious that Ice was following something intently, as she studied the coffee cup in her hand. The earphone was just barely protruding from her ear. "Is that Bluetooth?"

"They're all connected right now," Alfred explained. "It helps them to keep track of who is where."

"But Noah isn't," she cried out, looking at them in horror. "Nobody knows where Noah is. He didn't have that."

"No," Alfred said. "But remember, they did go to help him."

"Sure," she said, "but Noah lost his, when he and I left the truck. And, when the bomb went off, Noah took off, wanting to chase this guy down."

"The team knows that," he said. "They won't shoot their own man."

"No, no, of course not," she said, trying to calm her breathing. She swallowed hard and looked over at Ice. "I need to do something. Is there anything I can do to help?"

She looked over, smiled, and said, "No, really nothing you can do to help at the moment." She looked over at

Alfred and said, "I'm going downstairs." She smiled at Di. "You just stay here and rest. I'll be back up in a few minutes." She got up and strode away, but her footsteps were purposeful, determined.

"Where's she going?" Di cried out. Alfred hesitated. She looked at him. "Please don't lie to me."

"She's going to the medical center to make sure it's prepped and ready," he murmured.

"So somebody's been shot?"

"We don't know that. What we do know is that, if she's prepped, then if anyone does get injured, she's ready."

"Okay," she said, staring at him, trying to remember all the things that she'd heard about Ice's medical abilities. "Do you have a doctor here?"

"Not technically in residence, no, but what we have is probably better," he said. "Ice was a navy field medic. Several other people are heavily trained, and we have lots of staff with skills that far surpass a normal medical scenario. Ice can fly one of our helicopters, if someone needs to go to the hospital for emergency surgery or something equally traumatizing."

Dianne relaxed at that. "I keep forgetting how well equipped the compound is."

"And it's just for things like this," he said, "on the off chance that something goes wrong and that people need help. Levi and Ice always make sure their team is taken care of."

Di nodded, finding herself relaxing a little bit. "I know," she said, "but those bullets, they kill."

"They do," he said, "but I can't even begin to tell you how many bullets we've pulled out of guys here. Lots of times the bullets don't kill."

She smiled. "Have you been hauled in to help her?"

"I've done plenty of surgeries with her, particularly in the beginning," he said, with a big grin. "I was a field medic myself, way back when."

"You must have had a wonderful life," she murmured, studying him. He was older than Levi and Ice, but she understood that the couple had a military career together that went way back.

"Absolutely," he said. "And it's not ending anytime soon."

And such a twinkle was in his eye that she realized how she had worded it. She flushed. "I'm so sorry. I didn't mean to insult you."

"Don't you worry about it," he said, once again patting her hand.

What a soothing motion it was, and he'd been doing it periodically since she'd arrived. Whether it was supposed to calm her or him down was the question, but it seemed to be working. She smiled. "You're a very nice man."

"Thanks, I think," he said, and then he chuckled.

"I meant it nicely," she said, with a shrug. "It's always hard to know what to say to people sometimes."

"Hey, these aren't circumstances that most people have a chance to repeat," he said. "It's best to be natural and normal and honest at all times."

"I can do that," she said, with a smile. "After all, it's what I do on a regular basis."

"So, my understanding is," he said, "that you're in the health industry."

"I am," she said. "Whether it's a good place to be or not is the question," she said. "I was hoping to talk to Levi and Ice about it, about the potential to open a franchise store here."

"I'm no expert, but I can listen at least. What is the issue?"

"I'm looking for a business point of view, like what's happening in town and what the market looks like."

"More as a casual one-off kind of conversation?"

"Well, I certainly respect Ice's business ability," she said. "But, yeah, just as a curiosity, somebody to banter it back and forth. They're the ones who suggested it a long time ago."

"Well, if they suggested it, I'm pretty sure they think it's a good idea."

"And so do I," she said, "if all this hasn't changed my mind. It makes me feel odd to think of coming here now."

~

NOAH MIGHT NOT have been in the same spot, but he still felt the tug of the bullet as it caught his shirt. He fired off one shot in the direction of the rifle and heard an almost silent *oomph*. But it didn't sound bad enough to have stopped the gunman. Noah sent off several more, moving through the softening darkness as fast as he could, trying to move without making a sound, which was almost a lost cause out here. More gunfire sprayed in his direction, and he hit the ground, as the bullets zoomed overhead. He needed to get in closer, but this guy, with his semiautomatic rifle, was covering the area heavily with spray.

If Noah had any way to communicate with the others, he could have told them, although this gunfire would bring them all running. He knew that some of his team were here already, but now they all would converge. He stayed quiet, searching the ground around him. But, in this darkness and now the all-encompassing fog, it was almost impossible to discern movements. He knew roughly where the gunman was because Noah had seen the flash of the muzzle, but the shooter could have already moved ten feet by now.

Skittering on his belly, Noah moved forward about four feet, then took a chance at another yard or so. There was a rock, not big enough to really hide behind but enough that he could blend into, and he shifted closer, studying the terrain, finding nothing to help him discern anybody. Either the guy was prone on the ground, or he'd already disappeared. There was no grass, no trees, no brush to hide in around here. It looked like it was completely wide open. Noah saw one lone rock off to the side, and it was a little bit bigger than the one Noah had been hiding behind earlier.

He hesitated, wondering if he should try to reach it, when suddenly the rock looked like it was breathing. He froze and smiled. It was a cool move because the gunman had managed to blend into the rest of the terrain, and nobody would actually know it was a person rather than a rock. And he had done it so well that it was very convincing.

Noah studied the figure, wondering if it was the predator or if it was one of his own team. He assumed it was the gunman he was after, and, when he caught a shift of movement, and the rifle was lifted and pointed in another direction, ready to fire, Noah lifted his handgun and fired once. The man groaned, immediately turned in Noah's direction, spraying the ground with bullets. The gunman had already rolled off to the side, but Noah knew that he wouldn't have another chance if he didn't take this guy out now.

He fired twice more, racing forward from the side, even as the gunman took both body hits, shifting to the ground, his rifle firing into the air, as he tried to swing it up and around. Just as the muzzle neared Noah, facing him, Noah kicked out with his boot and caught it, shifting the angle so the bullets missed him. Or at least he hoped they did. He felt a tug on his thigh, but he couldn't worry about it, as he was coming down hard, his fist connecting with the predator's jaw, again and again and again.

Finally the man offered no more resistance and lay flat on the ground. Noah took a long slow deep breath, picked up his phone, and sent out an immediate call for help. Using Flashlight mode on his cell, he checked out the man's face and froze. This wasn't Maxwell, not unless he was in a damn good disguise. Noah quickly sent an image to Levi and checked the gunman over, when he felt a cold hard muzzle up against his back.

"Thought it was just me, didn't you?" said the stranger with a laugh.

Noah froze and swore silently in his head. They had always assumed it was just the one guy. And that was the problem; don't ever assume. "Who's this guy then?" Noah asked Maxwell.

"A hired gun. Somebody to give me a hand and to work as a decoy."

"Did he know you set him up as bait?"

"He knew what the score was," he said. "Nobody is innocent in this life."

"Well, some are," he said. "Some definitely are."

"BS," he snapped. "Everybody deserves to die."

"Well, everybody *will* die," Noah said. The gun nudged him harder, and he wondered what his chances were of pivoting, grabbing the gun, and taking it away. Probably not very good. He was looking at a bullet through the chest for sure. He had already sent out the call to Levi, knew they would locate his position, but he could only hope that somebody was coming real soon. Yet it was also a matter of making sure nobody came in too fast because, if that were the case, this guy would start shooting, and somebody would get hurt.

"Did you kill him?" Maxwell asked.

"No, your patsy's not dead," Noah said.

"Stand up," he said.

Noah slowly stood and shifted away from the body beside him. He also aligned himself sideways against the gun muzzle.

Maxwell looked down at his partner. "Too bad," he said. And before Noah had a chance to even react, the man fired one bullet into his partner's head.

Stunned, Noah snapped, "Did you have to kill him?"

"Absolutely. He was almost dead anyway. He should be thanking me." Maxwell stared at Noah, with a toothy grin. "But you?" he said. "You don't get to die quite so fast."

"Really?" Noah said, eyeing him carefully. He could take one bullet, maybe two, depending on how artfully they were placed. But after that it would be much harder to survive. He shifted on the balls of his feet.

"Yeah, I have to incapacitate you first." Maxwell shrugged. "You will be the bait that brings Levi in."

"Thanks for that," Noah said. "No problem."

Splat!

A bullet slammed into his leg. Noah swore, and, since it was the leg he had most of his weight on, he went down. He immediately tried to stop the bleeding, his hands pressing hard on the wound, as he stared up at the gunman. "Great," he said. "So now that I'm wounded, what now?"

"Levi will come in and try to rescue you," Maxwell said, with an airy wave of his hand. "After all, it's what he does."

"Right," Noah murmured. "And how do you know he even has a clue what's going on?" The trouble was, Maxwell was right. Levi would come. Noah just had to wait for the right moment to take out this asshole. Even with the bullet in his leg, no way Noah would let this guy live.

The man laughed. "Judging by the look in your eyes right now," he said, "if you had a chance, you'd wrap those hands of yours around my neck and squeeze until I couldn't breathe anymore."

"Well, you did just shoot me," Noah said, grinning through the pain.

"Yep, and if you don't shut up and be good," he said, "I'll shoot you again." And, with that, Maxwell turned to look around at the general area and called out, "Hey, Levi. Your sitting duck is here. I took him out with a bullet in the leg," he said. "If you don't show yourself, I'll put one in his head too." There was only silence all around.

Noah knew that Levi's motto was never to play the hostage game. And, even as Maxwell continued to scan the area, Noah shifted restlessly on the ground, making his shooter spin to look at him. But Noah was just trying to move his injured leg into a more comfortable position.

"Don't try anything," Maxwell warned.

"What am I supposed to try?" Noah asked.

At that, Maxwell laughed and nodded. "That's right," he said. "You're mine now." He turned and yelled back out, "Levi, get your ass over here. Ten minutes and I start popping him."

At that, Noah's blood ran cold. He looked around for a weapon. He'd been disarmed of his handgun, and it was at

Maxwell's feet, not very far away. That might be worth reaching for, but, as he put his hand down to shift the weight off his leg again—which was really booming with pain now—he noted rocks were all around here. He quickly slipped a half dozen into his pocket, moving silently. With one in his right hand, he waited for his chance.

As soon as another five minutes had gone by, Maxwell let out another roar into the darkness. "Levi, you got five minutes left." And he lifted his semiautomatic in the air and said, "If you don't believe me, look what I've got."

Since the gun was over Maxwell's head, Noah took aim, and, with one of the biggest rocks, he pitched it as hard as he could into the air and right at the man's temple. Adrenaline then drove Noah forward, helping to black out the devastating pain in his leg.

As Maxwell stumbled to the left, stunned by the rock, Maxwell was up in a flash and over at Noah's side, bringing the rifle down, even as Noah grabbed the end and butted him hard in the face with it, then hit him hard again with two more heavy slams to the jaw. Even as he finished the second one, he was suddenly surrounded by Levi and the team.

Maxwell groaned, as he shifted to his knees and then lunged with a knife, trying to attack Noah, Maxwell's focus only on Noah now, but he easily dodged the knife.

Levi tried to get his attention. "I'm here," he said. "Now what the hell do you want?"

"I want this asshole," Maxwell said, desperately trying to strike at Noah.

But again Noah slammed the gun butt hard against Maxwell's chest, sending the older man back, coughing now. "You're not taking me out. A bullet in my leg is one thing,"

Noah said, "but taking me down permanently is something entirely different." He kicked his own handgun away from the guy, in case he thought he would pick it up. With the others now taking over control, the gunman continued to cough several times, then heavier.

Nothing was normal about that cough. Noah looked over at Levi, who studied Maxwell curiously.

"What's that, lung cancer?" Levi asked.

"Stage four," Maxwell said, spitting out a great big chunk of something nasty looking onto the ground. There was enough light to see but not clearly "Shoot me. I don't care," he said. "I'm dead anyway."

"So, you chose to spend your last few months full of hate?" Levi asked. "Your last few months trying to hurt others, instead of enjoying what little life you had left?"

"There's no enjoying life when you've lost the only thing you care about," he snapped.

"You could have made a different choice," Levi said.

"There is no different choice. This is it. Go ahead and shoot me," he said. "It'll save me the last few months of pain."

"No, we won't do that," he said. "When it comes to pain, that's for you to bear. I'm a little tired of you bothering innocent friends of mine."

"She wasn't innocent," he said. "And she was just a means to an end anyway. What do I care? She's just another person out there. One of many who have hurt me over the years."

"Dianne didn't hurt you or your son. Neither did any of my friends. Yet, instead of spending the last few months trying to find something good in life, all you're doing is pouring hate and revenge and acid onto your soul."

"My soul's already rotten," he said. "There's no salvation for me." He looked up at Noah. "And you're the asshole who kept interfering," he said. "I should have shot you in the chest."

"You should have. I know I hit you a couple times."

"Yeah, but I've got on a bulletproof vest," he said, laughing. And, with that, he pulled the knife toward him. "And I'm not dropping this either."

"Well, we can't move you with it in your hand," Levi said.

"It's fine. I said you could just shoot me."

"Not happening."

He looked up at Levi and said, "Well, I'm not going to jail either." And with a movement that completely stunned Noah, Maxwell slammed the knife into his own throat.

Immediately gurgling sounds erupted, as blood gushed out, and air escaped. They rushed forward to stop the bleeding, but it was already too late. He had managed to not only stab in but had also pulled down, slicing an artery. It was over within seconds.

Noah looked over at Levi. "That's a hell of a way to end this."

"It is, indeed." Levi looked back at the second man. "What happened here?"

"Maxwell murdered him, his own patsy. I took him down, but this guy finished the job."

Levi said, "We'll have to bring the cops in on this one. It's all related to the attacks at the hotel." He looked over at Noah. "You better go see Ice. Can you walk?"

"Of course I can walk," he said, already ripping off his T-shirt and binding up his leg.

"Maybe not," Levi said, studying him. "You're looking

pale."

"Bullshit," Noah said, but, when he gauged how far he had to walk, he started to swear. "Goddammit," he said, "that's got to be a couple miles."

Levi laughed. "Absolutely," he said, "but we'll give you a hand."

"I'll do it," Noah said, and he limped his way toward the road.

Chapter 15

WHEN THE VEHICLE came flying into the compound, Di raced to the door, along with Ice. And, sure enough, Rory and Logan were carrying Noah.

"Oh my God," Di said. "What happened?"

"Gunshot wound," Rory murmured. "Looks like it missed the bone. It's his leg, just above the knee by a couple inches."

Ice immediately took command of the situation. "Get him downstairs," she said.

They carried him through to the clinic, and, although Di wasn't in any way helpful, she couldn't leave him, and she followed the entire troop. She stood off to the side ever-so-slightly, as she watched Ice go to work. "If there's anything I can do," she said hesitantly, "let me know."

"Come up here and hold his hand," Ice ordered her. "He's unconscious, but he needs to know that you're here."

"I don't have a problem doing that, but what difference will it make to him?"

"When we're unconscious, we're still in a state that allows us to know what goes on around us. People tend to do much better if the people they love are there."

"Oh." She didn't say anything to that. "Do you really think he cares? We only just met a matter of days ago."

"How would you doubt it?" she said. "You haven't had

much time together, but, in all honesty, that's been very normal for the rest of my team here too."

"What the hell is it that you've got going on here?"

"No idea," she said, "but it appears to be magic."

"Well, for some people it is."

Ice looked up briefly and gave her a warm smile. "I'd say welcome to the family, but I'm not sure you're ready to hear that yet."

Di just stared at her in astonishment. "No, I don't think I am. I mean, I get that something is between us, but—"

"You'll work it out," Ice said comfortably. "Don't believe me if you don't want to," she said, "but one question. Is he holding your hand back?"

Di nodded slowly. "There is some strength in his grip. As if he's there but maybe under layers and layers of pain."

"That's a good way to look at it," she said, "but it means he knows you're here."

"He'd be doing this with anybody's hand," she said, but just then her hand was squeezed even more. "Or maybe not." She leaned over, gently brushed his hair off his hot sweaty face. She squeezed Noah's fingers gently, her other hand reaching up to stroke his cheek and his neck. "Will he be okay?" she said, keeping her eyes averted from the blood.

"Yep," Ice said.

Di checked out the thigh wound and then winced. "That looks terrible."

"Well, it's not so bad here. See? It went in at an angle, missing the bone, so it's a flesh wound at this point," she said. "A good one but it went through, so it could have been much worse."

"Meaning?"

"Meaning that he's lucky," she said cheerfully.

"Doesn't look like he's lucky," Dianne whispered.

"Nope, he's good," she said. "A few stitches, then clean it all up, and he'll be good to go."

"He can't walk on that though, right?"

"Not for a while yet, no," Ice said. "But he won't need to go to the hospital."

"Well, that's good," Di said, with relief. And, when she thought about it, she said, "That's amazing actually. Do you do all the medical here?"

"I do a lot of it. We determine how bad it is, and, if they need to go in, they go in. But most of the guys here don't like hospitals, so we avoid it if we can." Ice looked up at her. "Speaking of that, don't you have some stitches that need attention?"

"Just a few, and they'll need to come out at some point. I didn't realize not going to the hospital was an option," she said. "When I was ... attacked, Noah ordered me into the hospital and then again when I was drugged."

Ice looked at Di, chuckled, and said, "Yeah, but you weren't knowledgeable enough at the time to actually stop Noah from forcing you to go."

"Well, that's true. Besides, I don't think he would have listened."

"Nope, not likely," Ice murmured. Finally she stepped back and, with a clean cloth, washed up the rest of his leg and then the rest of his body. Straightening, she said, "He's good to go."

"Whatever that means," Di said. She looked at the leg and said, "Wow, with the bandage on, it doesn't look too bad at all."

"Nope, it's all a matter of minimizing the damage going forward. He has to rest and make sure it's not getting infected."

"What's that mean? *Bed* rest?"

At that, Noah opened his eyes. "Like hell." He glared at Ice.

She glared right back. "Three days," she said, "*in bed.*"

He shook his head. "Not happening."

She reached down, tapped him lightly on the chin. "That's an order." And, with that, she turned and walked out.

He glared as she left and tried to sit up immediately. Di pushed him back down again. "Don't you start with me," she snapped. "We went to hell and back, waiting for them to get you out of the shoot-out."

He looked at her, smiled, and said, "Worried you, did I?"

She rolled her eyes at him. "You're not starting that."

"Why not?" And then his gaze turned crafty. "I know one way to keep me in bed."

When she caught his meaning, she burst out laughing and then flushed bright red. "Oh, no, you don't," she said, shaking her head. "If you're injured, you're injured."

"I'm not *that* injured," he said, waggling his eyebrows.

She snorted. "What the hell is wrong with you guys? You're not superhuman."

"No, but we do understand the value of life because so often we come up against death," he said quietly.

She frowned as she thought about it and then nodded. She leaned forward, kissed him on the cheek, and said, "I'm very happy to see that you'll be okay."

"I am too," he said, as he grabbed the back of her neck and pulled her inexorably closer. "But if you'll kiss me ..."

And this time he pulled her down, where he could kiss her

properly.

Flushed and heated, her body now felt something far more than she had ever expected. She looked at him.

"Like I said," he murmured, stroking her bottom lip with his thumb. "I could handle three days in bed, if I'm not alone."

She flushed. "That's not fair," she said, "and, besides, Ice wouldn't let you."

"Hell, Ice may not let me," he said, "but Levi would."

At that, she burst out laughing. "You know what? That's probably quite true," she said.

"Besides, don't you think Ice has any idea how this works?" he murmured. "She's used to us."

"Maybe," Di admitted, "but I'm not."

"You'll get used to it," he said. "We just need to give you a little bit longer."

"What's a little bit longer?" she asked.

"Three days, starting now," he said. "I'm not kidding about going up to my room."

"Shouldn't you wait here for somebody to help you?"

"Nope," he said. He shifted, sitting up.

He looked a little shaky, so she immediately stepped closer and put an arm around him. "Here. Let me help you."

He grinned down on her. "I don't think that'll work too well."

"I can be a big help," she said.

"I'm sure you can. We'll take the elevator up to my room."

"Your room?"

"Yep." He hopped up and stood on his good leg. He swore and said, "There's really no hope for it. I'll have to put some weight on it."

"No, you're not," she said, and she rushed over and grabbed crutches.

He nodded and said, "I wasn't thinking about that." But, with crutches under his arms, they made their way to the elevator and straight up to his room. By the time he made it to his bed, she saw the sweat on his brow.

"You need to lie down and rest," she exclaimed. "You heard the boss. *Three days.* Three days *in bed.* Before you know it, they'll be over."

But she was wrong. He was not a good patient and didn't appreciate being locked up for three days. By the time the second day rolled around, she was losing patience.

"Just go," he said. "You don't have to sit here and babysit me."

"Good," she said, "because that's what I *wasn't* doing in the first place."

He just glared at her and threw himself backward on the bed.

"Why are you so cranky anyway?"

At that, he didn't even bother answering; he just waved his hand at her.

"Well," she said, standing there, glaring at him, "I know you're hurt and all."

"I'm fine."

"But that's no reason for being grumpy or for this bad behavior."

He snorted.

She laughed. "Now who's being the sad puss?"

"Hey," he said, "I'm injured."

"Oh, so now you're injured," she said, rolling her eyes at him. She walked over and sat down on the side of the bed. "If you're bored, what do you want to do?"

"Not a whole lot I can do," he grumped.

"True," she said. "Okay, I'll just leave you to it." As she went to stand up, he reached out and grabbed her hand.

"Sit."

"I'm not a dog," she muttered.

"Please sit," he said, "and visit for a bit."

"I haven't been visiting?"

He shrugged.

She smiled, looked down at him, and said, "You're acting like a two-year-old." He glared at her. She leaned over, kissed him on the nose, and said, "Okay, so maybe a fourteen-year-old."

He rolled his eyes at that. "That's hardly any better."

"Maybe not," she said, "but I get that you don't like being sidelined."

"Nope, I sure don't."

"How long will she keep you off work?"

"A long time," he said.

"Oh, sorry."

"It is what it is," he said, "but I'd rather be out by the pool."

"Well, you could ask her if that's doable."

"If she says three days in bed, you can bet it'll be three days in bed."

"I see a lot of respect for Ice and for what she says."

"She's usually right," he said. "I just don't particularly like it."

"Well, I'm surprised it's three days. I would have thought forty-eight hours would have been enough."

"Me too, unless of course she thought this would need a longer recovery time for some reason." He rolled over, staring at her.

She saw the thoughts rolling around in his head.

Then he started to grin. "Or *something*."

She raised an eyebrow. "What do you mean?"

"Oh, I'm pretty damn sure that she said three days because of you."

She stared at him uncomprehendingly. "What?"

He tugged her down, so she was flat across his chest. "I'm pretty sure she's matchmaking."

"You're injured," she protested. "You can't fool around in bed."

"I sure as hell can," he said in astonishment.

She stared at him, couldn't let the idea go. Curiously she asked, "Really?"

He grinned. "Absolutely."

"*Hmm.* I wonder about that," she said.

"Don't need to wonder," he replied, touching her gently under the chin. "Anytime you're ready."

"What's it got to do with *me* being ready?" she asked. "You're the injured one."

"If you're waiting for me," he said, "I'm more than 100 percent ready to give this thing a roll."

"I don't want you hurt," she said immediately. "It's not good for you. It will stress your system."

"Like hell," he said succinctly.

She burst out laughing. "That is not at all what Ice intended. She wanted you to rest."

"I'm here. I'm completely rested," he said, flopping back on the bed, his arms wide.

And, true enough, he seemed perfectly fit. As evidenced by his body on display, since he wore only shorts and nothing else. She studied him, feeling her curiosity and a whole lot more warming inside. She shook her head. "No."

"What's holding you back?"

"You're injured."

"If that's the only reason," he said, shaking his head, "we can fix that immediately."

"No," she said, "we can't."

"Unless you don't want to."

She frowned at him. "This is awkward," she said.

"Oh, you know something? You're right," he said. He tugged her forward and asked, "How about this instead?" And he kept tugging her until she sprawled across his chest, and, grasping the sides of her head gently, he pulled her toward him.

She just waited while his lips claimed hers, and it was the same damn magic she'd felt before. When he finally lifted his head, she said, "You're deadly."

"No," he said, "we're deadly together. It doesn't always happen like this," he whispered and kissed her again, then again and again.

By the time she came up for air, her shirt was gone and so were her pants. She stared at herself, down to panties and a bra. "How the hell did you do that?"

He gave her a smug look. "Practice."

She shook her head. "I don't ever want to hear about that again."

He shook his head. "Doesn't have to be a bad thing," he said. "I spent all that time just getting it right." He pulled her gently into his arms.

"I still don't want to hurt you," she whispered.

"You won't," he said. "I promise." But she still frowned. He smiled a knowing smile, and she realized she was as nude as he was. She sat up on the side of the bed and stared at him. "Wow." Scars and bruises were all over his heavily-muscled body. She reached out a gentle finger. "This doesn't look very good."

"It's healing," he said, dismissing it. "That's what they all look like when they're healing."

She looked at him. "Really?"

He nodded. "Absolutely."

She leaned over and gave it a kiss, and then another one and another one. And he lay here, gently accepting everything she did. She realized just how much power there was in that moment. She kissed him again and again, her fingers and hands slowly exploring his body. The ribs, the muscles between the ribs, the six-pack under her hand, as she stroked gently down to his belly button. She dropped kisses on his bruises, kisses on his scars.

"If you want to keep that up," he said, "all of me is bruised and scarred up."

"I'll get there," she murmured tugging on his boxers. He obligingly lifted his hips for her to remove the offending cloth. She brushed her hair along his chest and his erection—standing up, ready for her attention. She gently dropped kisses on the edge and down the side of it. He shuddered beneath her, giving her an even greater glimpse at the power she held over him, as he remained completely open to her touch. She whispered, "I don't think it's ever been like this. Most guys don't like to let me take control."

His eyes flew open. "I do," he said. "Do whatever you want."

"Really?" she asked, in delight and curiosity.

He immediately nodded. "Absolutely," he said, "I'm here for your pleasure."

She smiled. "You might regret that."

"I might," he said. Then he grinned. "Remember though

that turnabout is fair play."

She nodded. "I can handle that."

"I wonder."

She lowered her head and took his erection into her mouth, gently teasing the end with her tongue, while he shuddered beneath her. His hips lifted in an instinctive movement, as old as time. She ran her hands up and down the length of him, before sliding them inside his thighs and around, coming up under his buttocks and across to his chest.

Finally she couldn't stand it any longer, and she slid up his chest, kissing every inch of the way, until she got to his lips, where she pulled his lower lip into her mouth and suckled gently. All the while she straddled his member and slowly lowered herself down. "I don't want to hurt your leg," she whispered.

"Good thing the bandage is far enough away then, isn't it?"

She looked back and realized the wound was a good twelve inches away. "You have to lie still," she said.

He rolled his eyes. "I'm trying."

She grinned. "No *trying* allowed. You have to succeed. Otherwise we'll get in trouble."

He burst out laughing. "I'm pretty sure this will help me heal more than anything time will do for it."

"I don't know about that," she said. And she slowly raised herself up, as if she would leave.

He immediately grabbed her hips and said, "No."

She smiled and said, "I wasn't going anywhere," and slowly sank back down again. And then she raised herself and sank. And finally she leaned forward, pushing herself deeper onto his member and asked, "Do you like to ride?"

"I love it," he said, his voice deep, dark, and smoky. "I hope you do too."

And that's what she did. With her head back, and her eyes closed, she rode, driving them both to the edge, before she found herself falling, as her climax ripped through her. He grabbed her hips and plunged upward once, twice, and then he groaned with his own orgasm. She sank on top of him and took a deep breath, trying to regain control.

"You can do that to me anytime you like," he whispered.

She looked down, kissed him gently and said, "I'm not so sure about that, since it damn-near killed me after all."

"It's all right," he said. "We'll get better at lasting longer with practice."

She burst out laughing, and he just grinned. "Will we always laugh like this?" she asked.

"I hope so," he said, his tone serious. "It's essential to both of us."

"It's so unusual," she said.

"Maybe so, but hopefully not for us."

"Is there an *us*?"

He looked at her, tilted up her chin, and said, "The very fact that you are here right now says there is definitely an us. And it's up to us what we do with it from here on out."

"I don't want it to be short and fast and over."

"Nobody said it would be," he murmured. "There's too much good in what we have."

"I haven't had too much experience with healthy relationships," she whispered.

"I have, of the friendship type," he said, "but I've been looking for the right romantic one for a very long time."

"Am I it?" she asked, wonder in her tone.

He smiled, nodded, and pulled her to him. "Absolutely.

You just have to believe."

"And if I can't?"

"I'll show you how," he said gently. And he brought her closer and kissed her, until she was completely mindless with passion again.

"You make me stupid when you do that," she murmured.

He chuckled. "Then I'll just have to keep doing that until you can see the light."

She smiled. "I think I'm already there."

"Not yet," he said, pulling her, so she was higher up in the bed, and he could roll over on his good side, his hand immediately sliding between her thighs. "But we'll get you there."

She wrapped her arms around his neck and whispered, "As long as you're holding me," she said, "I'll be fine."

"I promise," he said, "we'll be side by side the whole time."

She looked up at him in wonder.

"Do you promise?" he asked her.

"I promise." And this time, when he lowered his head, she sank into the dreamland he had shown her. "I can't wait."

It was everything she had ever wanted and so much more.

Epilogue

LEVI SAT IN the kitchen. "What do you think about this guy?" he asked Ice, dropping a file in front of her. She flipped it open, looked at it, and said, "Tomas. I brought up his name last year."

"Why didn't we go with him then?"

"Because, just after I talked to him, he was injured."

"What's his status now?"

"Let me find out." She pulled out her phone and called him. "Tomas, how are you doing?" A strong male voice came through her cell, and she put it on Speakerphone.

"I'm doing well," he said. "How are you?"

"I'm doing good. We're looking for some more men."

"Oh, hell," he said. "I figured I would be out of the running for good after the last accident."

"Tell us about it," Levi interjected.

~

TOMAS STARED AT the phone. "A revenge scenario," he said. "I was shot on a mission."

"Fully recovered?"

"No," he said, not pulling any punches. "I'll always walk with a bit of a limp."

"Anything else?"

"Isn't that enough?"

"Nope," Levi said. "If there's nothing but a limp, I'm good with that. Are you still a weapons specialist?"

"For anything I've had a chance to work on, yes," he said, "but I've been out of touch with anything for the last six—or make that eight—months."

"That's fine," he said. "We're looking for somebody to take over. One of our people who handles the arsenal in the compound is pregnant."

"Pregnant?" Tomas shook his head at that. "You have a woman there?"

"Several, but Kai is pregnant, and we're changing her duties around a bit."

"Makes sense to me. Is this full-time or part-time?" he asked. "I never expected to be asked to take over for maternity leave."

Levi burst out laughing. "Well, you should be honored in this case, if you get the opportunity," he said.

"So, what do I have to do? Try out or something?"

"Not so sure about that," he said, "but we do have a job, and if you want to go as a spare," he said, "we'll see how it works out."

"I can do that," he said.

"Are you on any medication?" Ice asked.

"Nope, just came off the last of them about two weeks ago."

"And what were they for?"

"Blood thinners. I was having too many blood clotting issues."

"Interesting," she murmured. "But, as long as you're healthy enough, and you think you're ready to give it a run, we're more than ready to give you a shot."

"Perfect. What's the job?"

They both hesitated. Levi looked over at her, shrugged, and said, "We might as well tell him."

"Tell me what?" Tomas asked curiously. "I really don't like going into anything if I don't know what I'm dealing with."

"That's fair," she said. "We have news of a supremacy group that's collecting weapons."

"Where?"

"Just outside of Houston actually," he said. "We don't get too many local jobs, and we have a lot of people who want to do this one. So we do have men available, but we just thought it might be an opportunity to see how you handle things."

"If you say so," he said, "I'm up for it."

"Whereabouts are you right now?"

"I'm in Dallas," he said, "so I can be in Houston in a few hours."

"Good. I'll set you up at a hotel with an alias to check in."

"A hotel?"

"Yep, you'll be joining the group as a friend of a woman already part of the group. Amber contacted us a couple days ago. She joined to help free her friend from it, but that friend is now dead, and Amber's looking for help. Not just to get out herself but to burn the group to the ground."

"Ah, undercover then. That's perfect. You got a story for me?"

"Yep, I do," he said, "and it's a doozy. If you're in, I'll send you the details in a minute."

"I am definitely in," he said, "particularly for bringing down something like this."

"Absolutely. Way too much of this shit going on in town

now."

"Send me the info. I'm packing already." And, with that, Tomas hung up, a smile on his face.

When Ice had called him before his accident, he'd been thrilled. He had been out of the navy for only two months and was at loose ends, trying to figure out what to do, when she had contacted him. But, sure as hell, he had ended up called back in because somebody had a grudge to settle, and Tomas had been the one who ended up in the middle. Now here he was, maybe, with a second chance. He was good with those. Particularly in this case.

He smiled a happy smile. Who the hell knew where this job would take him? Wherever that may be, he was more than ready for the journey. He'd had his fill of everything up until now and was just waiting to get back into the action. As he walked around his small apartment, his to-go bag in his hand, he took one final look.

I may or may not come back here, and that's just perfect.

And, with that thought, he walked out with a huge smile on his face.

This concludes Book 25 of Heroes for Hire:
Noah's Nemesis.
Read about Tomas's Trials: Heroes for Hire, Book 25

Heroes for Hire: Tomas's Trials (Book #26)

Tomas is excited about this new direction in his life. Working for Levi allows him to use his vast array of skills in new and varied ways. He doesn't expect to be sent undercover in a supremacy group, loaded with weapons. Yet what he finds is much more complicated than that.

Amber had joined the group to help get her friend away from the members, only to find out her friend is dead, and no one will talk about it. The group is in the middle of a coup from within, as the leader barely maintains control. It's a dangerous place to be, but she is not leaving without answers. Needing help, she contacts an old friend. Tomas isn't what she expects.

Still, as long as he will help her do what she needs to do—before she gets into further trouble—he is fine with her. Except it doesn't take long for both of them to realize that the danger is escalating to the point where it is possible that neither of them will leave the compound—at least not alive.

Find Book 26 here!

To find out more visit Dale Mayer's website.
http://smarturl.it/DMSTomas

Other Military Series by Dale Mayer

SEALs of Honor
Heroes for Hire
SEALs of Steel
The K9 Files
The Mavericks
Bullards Battle
Hathaway House
Terkel's Team

Ryland's Reach: Bullard's Battle (Book #1)

Welcome to a new stand-alone but interconnected series from Dale Mayer. This is Bullard's story—and that of his team's. All raw, rough, incredibly capable men who have one goal: to find out who was behind the attack on their leader, before the attacker, or attackers, return to finish the job.

Stay tuned for more nonstop action as the men narrow down their suspects … and find a way to let love back into their own empty lives.

His rescue from the ocean after a horrible plane explosion was his top priority, in any way, shape, or form. A small sailboat and a nurse to do the job was more than Ryland hoped for.

When Tabi somehow drags him and his buddy Garret onboard and surprisingly gets them to a naval ship close by, Ryland figures he'd used up all his luck and his friend's too. Sure enough, those who attacked the plane they were in weren't content to let him slowly die in the ocean. No. Surviving had made him a target all over again.

Tabi isn't expecting her sailing holiday to include the rescue of two badly injured men and then to end with the loss of her beloved sailboat. Her instincts save them, but now she finds it tough to let them go—even as more of Bullard's team members come to them—until it becomes apparent that not only are Bullard and his men still targets ... but she is too.

B ULLARD CHECKED THAT the helicopter was loaded with their bags and that his men were ready to leave.

He walked back one more time, his gaze on Ice. She'd never looked happier, never looked more perfect. His heart ached, but he knew she remained a caring friend and always would be. He opened his arms; she ran into them, and he held her close, whispering, "The offer still stands."

She leaned back and smiled up at him. "Maybe if and when Levi's been gone for a long enough time for me to forget," she said in all seriousness.

"That's not happening. You two, now three, will live long and happy lives together," he said, smiling down at the woman knew to be the most beautiful, inside and out. She would never be his, but he always kept a little corner of his heart open and available, in case she wanted to surprise him and to slide inside.

And then he realized she'd already been a part of his heart all this time. That was a good ten to fifteen years by now. But she kept herself in the friend category, and he understood because she and Levi, partners and now parents, were perfect together.

Bullard reached out and shook Levi's hand. "It was a hell of a blast," he said. "When you guys do a big splash, you really do a *big* splash."

Ice laughed. "A few days at home sounds perfect for me now."

"It looks great," he said, his hands on his hips as he surveyed the people in the massive pool surrounded by the palm trees, all designed and decked out by Ice. Right beside all the war machines that he heartily approved of. He grinned at her. "When are you coming over to visit?" His gaze went to Levi, raising his eyebrows back at her. "You guys should come over for a week or two or three."

"It's not a bad idea," Levi said. "We could use a long holiday, just not yet."

"That sounds familiar." Bullard grinned. "Anyway, I'm off. We'll hit the airport and then pick up the plane and head home." He added, "As always, call if you need me."

Everybody raised a hand as he returned to the helicopter and his buddy who was flying him to the airport. Ice had volunteered to shuttle him there, but he hadn't wanted to take her away from her family or to prolong the goodbye. He hopped inside, waving at everybody as the helicopter lifted. Two of his men, Ryland and Garret, were in the back seats. They always traveled with him.

Bullard would pick up the rest of his men in Australia. He stared down at the compound as he flew overhead. He preferred his compound at home, but damn they'd done a nice job here.

With everybody on the ground screaming goodbye, Bullard sailed over Houston, heading toward the airport. His two men never said a word. They all knew how he felt about Ice. But not one of them would cross that line and say anything. At least not if they expected to still have jobs.

It was one thing to fall in love with another man's woman, but another thing to fall in love with a woman who was so unique, so different, and so absolutely perfect that you knew, just knew, there was no hope of finding anybody else like her. But she and Levi had been together way before Bullard had ever met her, which made it that much more heartbreaking.

Still, he'd turned and looked forward. He had a full roster of jobs himself to focus on when he got home. Part of him was tired of the life; another part of him couldn't wait to head out on the next adventure. He managed to run everything from his command centers in one or two of his locations. He'd spent a lot of time and effort at the second one and kept a full team at both locations, yet preferred to spend most of his time at the old one. It felt more like home to him, and he'd like to be there now, but still had many more days before that could happen.

The helicopter lowered to the tarmac, he stepped out, said his goodbyes and walked across to where his private plane waited. It was one of the things that he loved, being a pilot of both helicopters and airplanes, and owning both birds himself.

That again was another way he and Ice were part of the same team, of the same mind-set. He'd been looking for another woman like Ice for himself, but no such luck. Sure, lots were around for short-term relationships, but most of them couldn't handle his lifestyle or the violence of the world that he lived in. He understood that.

The ones who did had a hard edge to them that he found difficult to live with. Bullard appreciated everybody's being alert and aware, but if there wasn't some softness in the women, they seemed to turn cold all the way through.

As he boarded his small plane, Ryland and Garret following behind, Bullard called out in his loud voice, "Let's go, slow pokes. We've got a long flight ahead of us."

The men grinned, confident Bullard was teasing, as was his usual routine during their off-hours.

"Well, we're ready, not sure about you though..." Ryland said, smirking.

"We're waiting on you this time," Garret added with a chuckle. "Good thing you're the boss."

Bullard grinned at his two right-hand men. "Isn't that the truth?" He dropped his bags at one of the guys' feet and said, "Stow all this stuff, will you? I want to get our flight path cleared and get the hell out of here."

They'd all enjoyed the break. He tried to get over once a year to visit Ice and Levi and same in reverse. But it was time to get back to business. He started up the engines, got confirmation from the tower. They were heading to Australia for this next job. He really wanted to go straight back to Africa, but it would be a while yet. They'd refuel in Honolulu.

Ryland came in and sat down in the copilot's spot, buckled in, then asked, "You ready?"

Bullard laughed. "When have you ever known me *not* to be ready?" At that, he taxied down the runway. Before long he was up in the air, at cruising level, and heading to Hawaii. "Gotta love these views from up here," Bullard said. "This place is magical."

"It is once you get up above all the smog," he said. "Why Australia again?"

"Remember how we were supposed to check out that newest compound in Australia that I've had my eye on? Besides the alpha team is coming off that ugly job in Sydney. We'll give them a day or two of R&R then head home."

"Right. We could have some equally ugly payback on that job."

Bullard shrugged. "That goes for most of our jobs. It's the life."

"And don't you have enough compounds to look after?"

"Yes I do, but that kid in me still looks to take over the world. Just remember that."

"Better you go home to Africa and look after your first two compounds," Ryland said.

"Maybe," Bullard admitted. "But it seems hard to not continue expanding."

"You need a partner," Ryland said abruptly. "That might ease the savage beast inside. Keep you home more."

"Well, the only one I like," he said, "is married to my best friend."

"I'm sorry about that," Ryland said quietly. "What a shit deal."

"No," Bullard said. "I came on the scene last. They were always meant to be together. Especially now they are a family."

"If you say so," Ryland said.

Bullard nodded. "Damn right, I say so."

And that set the tone for the next many hours. They landed in Hawaii, and while they fueled up everybody got off to stretch their legs by walking around outside a bit as this was a small private airstrip, not exactly full of hangars and tourists. Then they hopped back on board again for takeoff.

"I can fly," Ryland offered as they took off.

"We'll switch in a bit," Bullard said. "Surprisingly, I'm doing okay yet, but I'll let you take her down."

"Yeah, it's still a long flight," Ryland said studying the islands below. It was a stunning view of the area.

"I love the islands here. Sometimes I just wonder about the benefit of, you know, crashing into the sea, coming up on a deserted island, and finding the simple life again," Bullard said with a laugh.

"I hear you," Ryland said. "Every once in a while, I wonder the same."

Several hours later Ryland looked up and said abruptly, "We've made good time considering we've already passed Fiji."

Bullard yawned.

"Let's switch."

Bullard smiled, nodded, and said, "Fine. I'll hand it over to you."

Just then a funny noise came from the engine on the right side.

They looked at each other, and Ryland said, "Uh-oh. That's not good news."

Boom!

And the plane exploded.

Find Bullard's Battle (Book #1) here!
To find out more visit Dale Mayer's website.
smarturl.it/DMSRyland

Damon's Deal: Terkel's Team (Book #1)

Welcome to a brand-new series from *USA Today* best-selling author Dale Mayer, where dark-ops SEALs have special senses and skills, needed to solve intrigue, betrayal, and … murder. A series with all the elements you've come to love, plus so much more, … including psychics!

ICE POURED HERSELF a coffee and sat down at the compound's massive dining room table with the others. When her phone rang, she smiled at the number displayed. "Hey, Terk. How're you doing?" She put the call on Speakerphone.

"I'm okay," Terkel said, his voice distracted and tight.

"Terk?" Merk called from across the table. He got up and walked closer and sat across from Levi. "You don't sound too good, brother. What's up?"

"I'm fine," Terk said. "Or I will be. Right now, things are blown to shit."

"As in literally?" Merk asked.

"The entire group," Terk said, "they're all gone. I had a

solid team of eight, and they're all gone."

"Dead?"

Several others stood to join them, gathered around Ice's phone. Levi stepped forward, his hand on Ice's shoulder. "Terk? Are they all dead?"

"No." Terk took a deep breath. "I'm not making sense. I'm sorry."

"Take it easy," Ice said, her voice calm and reassuring. "What do you mean, *they're all gone?*"

"All their abilities are gone," he said. "Something's happened to them. Somebody has deliberately removed whatever super senses they could utilize—or what we have been utilizing for the last ten years for the government." His tone was bitter. "When the US gov recently closed us down, they promised that our black ops department would never rise again, but I didn't expect them to attack us personally."

"What are you talking about?" Merk said in alarm, standing up now to stare at Ice's phone. "Are you in danger?"

"Maybe? I don't know," Terk said. "I need to find out exactly what the hell's going on."

"What can we do to help?" Ice asked.

Terk gave a broken laugh. "That's not why I'm calling. Well, it is, but it isn't."

Ice looked at Merk, who frowned, as he shook his head. Ice knew he and the others had heard Terk's stressed out tone and the completely confusing bits and pieces coming from his mouth. Ice said, "Terk, you're not making sense again. Take a breath and explain. Please. You're scaring me."

Terk took a long slow deep breath. "Tell Stone to open the gate," he said. "She's out there."

"Who's out there?" Levi asked, hopped up, looked outside, and shrugged.

"She's coming up the road now. You have to let her in."

"Who? Why?"

"*Because*," he said, "she's also harnessed with C-4."

"Jesus," Levi said, bolting to display the camera feeds to the big screen in the room. "Is it live?"

"It is, and she's been sent to you."

"Well, that's an interesting move," Ice said, her voice sharp, activating her comm to connect to Stone in the control room. "Who's after us?"

"I think it's rebels within the Iranian government. But it could be our own government. I don't know anymore," Terk snapped. "I also don't know how they got her so close to you. Or how they pinned your connection to me," he said. "I've been very careful."

"We can look after ourselves," Ice said immediately. "But who is this woman to you?"

"She's pregnant," he said, "so that adds to the intensity here."

"Understood. So who is the father? Is he connected somehow?"

There was silence on the other end.

Merk said, "Terk, talk to us."

"She's carrying my baby," Terk replied, his voice heavy.

Merk, his expression grim, looked at Ice, her face mirroring his shock. He asked, "How do you know her, Terk?"

"Brother, you don't understand," Terk said. "I've never met this woman before in my life." And, with that, the phone went dead.

Find Terkel's Team (Book #1) here!

To find out more visit Dale Mayer's website.

smarturl.it/DMSTTDamon

Author's Note

Thank you for reading Noah's Nemesis: Heroes for Hire, Book 25! If you enjoyed the book, please take a moment and leave a short review.

Dear reader,

I love to hear from readers, and you can contact me at my website: www.dalemayer.com or at my Facebook author page. To be informed of new releases and special offers, sign up for my newsletter or follow me on BookBub. And if you are interested in joining Dale Mayer's Reader Group, here is the Facebook sign up page. https://smarturl.it/DaleMayerFBGroup

Cheers,
Dale Mayer

Your THREE Free Books Are Waiting!

Grab your copy of SEALs of Honor Books 1 – 3 for free!

Meet Mason, Hawk and Dane. *Brave, badass warriors who serve their country with honor and love their women to the limits of life and death.*

DOWNLOAD your copy right now! Just tell me where to send it.

www.smarturl.it/DaleHonorFreeBundle

About the Author

Dale Mayer is a *USA Today* best-selling author, best known for her SEALs military romances, her Psychic Visions series, and her Lovely Lethal Garden cozy series. Her contemporary romances are raw and full of passion and emotion (Broken But … Mending series). Her thrillers will keep you guessing (By Death series), and her romantic comedies will keep you giggling (*It's a Dog's Life*, a stand-alone novella; and the Broken Protocols series, starring Charming Marvin, the cat).

Dale honors the stories that come to her—and some of them are crazy and break all the rules and cross multiple genres!

To go with her fiction, she also writes nonfiction in many different fields, with books available on résumé writing, companion gardening, and the US mortgage system. She has recently published her Career Essentials series. All her books are available in print and ebook format.

Connect with Dale Mayer Online

Dale's Website – www.dalemayer.com
Twitter – @DaleMayer
Facebook – facebook.com/DaleMayer.author
BookBub – bookbub.com/authors/dale-mayer

Also by Dale Mayer

Published Adult Books:

Bullard's Battle
Ryland's Reach, Book 1
Cain's Cross, Book 2
Eton's Escape, Book 3
Garret's Gambit, Book 4
Kano's Keep, Book 5
Fallon's Flaw, Book 6
Quinn's Quest, Book 7
Bullard's Beauty, Book 8
Bullard's Best, Book 9

Terkel's Team
Damon's Deal, Book 1

Kate Morgan
Simon Says… Hide, Book 1

Hathaway House
Aaron, Book 1
Brock, Book 2
Cole, Book 3
Denton, Book 4

Elliot, Book 5
Finn, Book 6
Gregory, Book 7
Heath, Book 8
Iain, Book 9
Jaden, Book 10
Keith, Book 11
Lance, Book 12
Melissa, Book 13
Nash, Book 14
Owen, Book 15
Hathaway House, Books 1–3
Hathaway House, Books 4–6
Hathaway House, Books 7–9

The K9 Files
Ethan, Book 1
Pierce, Book 2
Zane, Book 3
Blaze, Book 4
Lucas, Book 5
Parker, Book 6
Carter, Book 7
Weston, Book 8
Greyson, Book 9
Rowan, Book 10
Caleb, Book 11
Kurt, Book 12
Tucker, Book 13

Harley, Book 14
The K9 Files, Books 1–2
The K9 Files, Books 3–4
The K9 Files, Books 5–6
The K9 Files, Books 7–8
The K9 Files, Books 9–10
The K9 Files, Books 11–12

Lovely Lethal Gardens
Arsenic in the Azaleas, Book 1
Bones in the Begonias, Book 2
Corpse in the Carnations, Book 3
Daggers in the Dahlias, Book 4
Evidence in the Echinacea, Book 5
Footprints in the Ferns, Book 6
Gun in the Gardenias, Book 7
Handcuffs in the Heather, Book 8
Ice Pick in the Ivy, Book 9
Jewels in the Juniper, Book 10
Killer in the Kiwis, Book 11
Lifeless in the Lilies, Book 12
Murder in the Marigolds, Book 13
Nabbed in the Nasturtiums, Book 14
Offed in the Orchids, Book 15
Lovely Lethal Gardens, Books 1–2
Lovely Lethal Gardens, Books 3–4
Lovely Lethal Gardens, Books 5–6
Lovely Lethal Gardens, Books 7–8
Lovely Lethal Gardens, Books 9–10

Psychic Vision Series

Tuesday's Child
Hide 'n Go Seek
Maddy's Floor
Garden of Sorrow
Knock Knock…
Rare Find
Eyes to the Soul
Now You See Her
Shattered
Into the Abyss
Seeds of Malice
Eye of the Falcon
Itsy-Bitsy Spider
Unmasked
Deep Beneath
From the Ashes
Stroke of Death
Ice Maiden
Snap, Crackle…
What If…
Psychic Visions Books 1–3
Psychic Visions Books 4–6
Psychic Visions Books 7–9

By Death Series

Touched by Death
Haunted by Death
Chilled by Death

By Death Books 1–3

Broken Protocols – Romantic Comedy Series
Cat's Meow
Cat's Pajamas
Cat's Cradle
Cat's Claus
Broken Protocols 1-4

Broken and... Mending
Skin
Scars
Scales (of Justice)
Broken but... Mending 1-3

Glory
Genesis
Tori
Celeste
Glory Trilogy

Biker Blues
Morgan: Biker Blues, Volume 1
Cash: Biker Blues, Volume 2

SEALs of Honor
Mason: SEALs of Honor, Book 1
Hawk: SEALs of Honor, Book 2
Dane: SEALs of Honor, Book 3
Swede: SEALs of Honor, Book 4

Shadow: SEALs of Honor, Book 5
Cooper: SEALs of Honor, Book 6
Markus: SEALs of Honor, Book 7
Evan: SEALs of Honor, Book 8
Mason's Wish: SEALs of Honor, Book 9
Chase: SEALs of Honor, Book 10
Brett: SEALs of Honor, Book 11
Devlin: SEALs of Honor, Book 12
Easton: SEALs of Honor, Book 13
Ryder: SEALs of Honor, Book 14
Macklin: SEALs of Honor, Book 15
Corey: SEALs of Honor, Book 16
Warrick: SEALs of Honor, Book 17
Tanner: SEALs of Honor, Book 18
Jackson: SEALs of Honor, Book 19
Kanen: SEALs of Honor, Book 20
Nelson: SEALs of Honor, Book 21
Taylor: SEALs of Honor, Book 22
Colton: SEALs of Honor, Book 23
Troy: SEALs of Honor, Book 24
Axel: SEALs of Honor, Book 25
Baylor: SEALs of Honor, Book 26
Hudson: SEALs of Honor, Book 27
SEALs of Honor, Books 1–3
SEALs of Honor, Books 4–6
SEALs of Honor, Books 7–10
SEALs of Honor, Books 11–13
SEALs of Honor, Books 14–16
SEALs of Honor, Books 17–19

SEALs of Honor, Books 20–22
SEALs of Honor, Books 23–25

Heroes for Hire

Levi's Legend: Heroes for Hire, Book 1
Stone's Surrender: Heroes for Hire, Book 2
Merk's Mistake: Heroes for Hire, Book 3
Rhodes's Reward: Heroes for Hire, Book 4
Flynn's Firecracker: Heroes for Hire, Book 5
Logan's Light: Heroes for Hire, Book 6
Harrison's Heart: Heroes for Hire, Book 7
Saul's Sweetheart: Heroes for Hire, Book 8
Dakota's Delight: Heroes for Hire, Book 9
Tyson's Treasure: Heroes for Hire, Book 10
Jace's Jewel: Heroes for Hire, Book 11
Rory's Rose: Heroes for Hire, Book 12
Brandon's Bliss: Heroes for Hire, Book 13
Liam's Lily: Heroes for Hire, Book 14
North's Nikki: Heroes for Hire, Book 15
Anders's Angel: Heroes for Hire, Book 16
Reyes's Raina: Heroes for Hire, Book 17
Dezi's Diamond: Heroes for Hire, Book 18
Vince's Vixen: Heroes for Hire, Book 19
Ice's Icing: Heroes for Hire, Book 20
Johan's Joy: Heroes for Hire, Book 21
Galen's Gemma: Heroes for Hire, Book 22
Zack's Zest: Heroes for Hire, Book 23
Bonaparte's Belle: Heroes for Hire, Book 24
Noah's Nemesis: Heroes for Hire, Book 25

Tomas's Trials: Heroes for Hire, Book 26
Heroes for Hire, Books 1–3
Heroes for Hire, Books 4–6
Heroes for Hire, Books 7–9
Heroes for Hire, Books 10–12
Heroes for Hire, Books 13–15

SEALs of Steel
Badger: SEALs of Steel, Book 1
Erick: SEALs of Steel, Book 2
Cade: SEALs of Steel, Book 3
Talon: SEALs of Steel, Book 4
Laszlo: SEALs of Steel, Book 5
Geir: SEALs of Steel, Book 6
Jager: SEALs of Steel, Book 7
The Final Reveal: SEALs of Steel, Book 8
SEALs of Steel, Books 1–4
SEALs of Steel, Books 5–8
SEALs of Steel, Books 1–8

The Mavericks
Kerrick, Book 1
Griffin, Book 2
Jax, Book 3
Beau, Book 4
Asher, Book 5
Ryker, Book 6
Miles, Book 7
Nico, Book 8

Keane, Book 9
Lennox, Book 10
Gavin, Book 11
Shane, Book 12
Diesel, Book 13
Jerricho, Book 14
Killian, Book 15
The Mavericks, Books 1–2
The Mavericks, Books 3–4
The Mavericks, Books 5–6
The Mavericks, Books 7–8
The Mavericks, Books 9–10
The Mavericks, Books 11–12

Collections
Dare to Be You...
Dare to Love...
Dare to be Strong...
RomanceX3

Standalone Novellas
It's a Dog's Life
Riana's Revenge
Second Chances

Published Young Adult Books:

Family Blood Ties Series
Vampire in Denial
Vampire in Distress

Vampire in Design
Vampire in Deceit
Vampire in Defiance
Vampire in Conflict
Vampire in Chaos
Vampire in Crisis
Vampire in Control
Vampire in Charge
Family Blood Ties Set 1–3
Family Blood Ties Set 1–5
Family Blood Ties Set 4–6
Family Blood Ties Set 7–9
Sian's Solution, A Family Blood Ties Series Prequel Novelette

Design series
Dangerous Designs
Deadly Designs
Darkest Designs
Design Series Trilogy

Standalone
In Cassie's Corner
Gem Stone (a Gemma Stone Mystery)
Time Thieves

Published Non-Fiction Books:

Career Essentials
Career Essentials: The Résumé

Career Essentials: The Cover Letter
Career Essentials: The Interview
Career Essentials: 3 in 1

Made in the USA
Monee, IL
08 September 2021